The Railway Man

The Railway Man

John Dean

ROBERT HALE · LONDON

© John Dean 2009
First published in Great Britain 2009

ISBN 978-0-7090-8915-5

Robert Hale Limited
Clerkenwell House
Clerkenwell Green
London EC1R 0HT

www.halebooks.com

The right of John Dean to be identified as author
of this work has been asserted by him in accordance with
the Copyright, Designs and Patents Act 1988

2 4 6 8 10 9 7 5 3 1

Typeset in 11/15pt New Century Schoolbook
Printed in Great Britain by the MPG Books Group, Bodmin and King's Lynn

chapter one

The Spur was ominously quiet when, shortly after midnight, the police patrol car edged its way across the estate's main quadrangle, its tyres crunching on broken glass. After it had slowed to a halt in the middle of the square, two uniformed police officers got out and stood in silence as they surveyed the scene. Loathe to leave the security of their vehicle, they allowed their gaze to roam along the darkened windows in the blocks of maisonettes that surrounded them. Still not speaking, they glanced at each other, each disturbed by the oppressive silence in the clammy summer night air. Everyone knew The Spur's reputation. Everyone knew what it could do to the unwary.

'This does not feel right,' said Gary Canham.

Brian Robertshaw said nothing. Aged in his mid fifties and less than a year from retirement, his experience counted for little as he caught something of the young constable's unease. The sergeant's mind went back to nightmarish nights spent on The Spur over the years, to the hatred he had seen in the eyes of its residents, to the murderous instincts that had long made it the most feared of the city's estates, to dancing fires illuminating the night and to hurled insults hanging in the air. Conscious now that the constable would be seeking leadership, Robertshaw tried not to let his unease show as slowly, very slowly, the two officers started to walk across the square, their eyes still seeking out any movement which could signal danger. Two floors above them, Tommy Rafferty stood in the stifling shadows of his flat, clutching a half-empty can of cheap lager in his hand and peering down through the gap in the curtains, his breathing heavy and laboured in the silence.

'Welcome to Hell, boys,' he wheezed and gave a dry, rasping laugh.

As ever, the effort made him cough and Rafferty stepped back into the room, fearful lest it be heard through the open window. The last thing Tommy Rafferty wanted was to get involved with the police. Not now. When he looked back into the square, the officers had disappeared from view and he assumed that they had reached one of the stairwells down below him. Careful lest he make another sound, Rafferty opened his window a little wider, wincing at the creaking which seemed to reverberate round the empty square. Moving carefully, he leaned out a little: if he listened hard, he could hear their every word on the still night air.

'How can people live here?' said Canham bleakly as he recoiled at the stench of stale urine coming from the stairwell. 'I mean, what happened to pride, Bri?'

'It wasn't always like this. Hey, don't look like that, it wasn't. I used to visit my granda here every weekend when I were a kid. There was a real sense of community in them days.'

'I'll have to take your word for it,' grunted Canham.

With a sour look on his face, he turned and let his gaze roam around the quadrangle once more. Constructed in the sixties, the estate comprised three identical squares, each one bordered by blocks of maisonettes. Like the others, the square was littered with broken bottles, used condoms and syringes and straggly weeds poked through cracks in the concrete. The blocks themselves were run down, many of the doors splintered and gashed, numerous windows boarded up and antipolice graffiti scrawled across the concrete balconies running round the edge of the quadrangle.

'What a dump,' said Canham.

'And one that's way too quiet,' murmured Robertshaw. 'There's no way that all this lot fancied a Friday night in with a good book and a Horlicks.'

The sergeant took a few steps back and glanced at the upper landings directly above him. Rafferty shrunk back into the shadows again.

'Are you sure this is where the truck came?' asked Canham.

'Control reckons one of the residents saw it arrive twenty minutes ago. It certainly matches the description of the flatbed seen near St Luke's.'

'I don't suppose this Good Samaritan gave a name?'

'What do you think?' said Robertshaw.

Canham nodded; they both knew that many of the decent people had long been driven out of The Spur and that those who remained lived in fear, too afraid to speak out against the drug dealers, petty criminals and alcoholics who were now their neighbours. Everyone knew what had happened here several years before. No one would ever forget it. Robertshaw had been one of the first officers on to the estate the night it happened and recalled the terrible events every time he ventured back on to the estate. All the officers in Hafton felt the same: it was what made The Spur unique.

Canham looked round at the scattering of dilapidated cars parked round the edges of the quadrangle: one of them was burnt out, another had its rear wheels missing and none of them had tax discs.

'I think this is a set-up,' he said, a fresh urgency in his voice as he gestured with his hand. 'I mean, where *is* the truck, Bri? I can't see it.'

'No,' replied Robertshaw, lips pursed, 'neither can I.'

A movement caught Canham's eye over to the left. Peering closer, the constable thought he could just make out a figure retreating into the darkness. Even though the figure vanished as rapidly as it had appeared, instinct told the young officer that The Spur was not the place to be.

'Time to leave,' said Canham.

'We can't,' replied Robertshaw firmly as he stepped into the stairwell, his voice echoing back out of the darkness. 'We have a job to do.'

Canham did not move. After a few seconds, Robertshaw reappeared.

'You coming?' he asked.

'Sorry,' said Canham, starting to walk back towards the patrol car. 'I'm not going to get my head stoved in for the sake of a bit of lead nicked from a church roof. Let the day shift sort it.'

Robertshaw tried to assume an authoritative air as he eyed the young officer.

'Now listen here, son,' he said, 'it's our job to—'

'Just like it was Kenny's?' said Canham sharply, then clapped a hand to his mouth. 'Sorry, uncalled for.'

Robertshaw said nothing, the comment having choked the words in his throat. Standing there in the stillness of the night, he recalled the fresh-faced young officer murdered on the estate several years previously. Called to investigate a report of a burglary, the PC had become separated from his colleague and been set upon by a gang of youths. In the mêlée that followed, a knife had flashed in the darkness and Kenny Jarvis had fallen. Images of his ready smile danced before Robertshaw's eyes and the sergeant felt the tears starting into his eyes, as always when he thought of that night.

The image of the body sprawled on the stairs, the blood seeping through his uniform, was followed by the thought of the sergeant's two teenaged daughters asleep in their beds, safe and peaceful in the knowledge that their father would be there when they awoke in the morning, bustling around in the kitchen, having just come off shift. 'Sleep tight, see you for breakfast,' he always said when he left the house for a night shift. But since the death of Kenny Jarvis, the thought that one day he would not see them for breakfast had loomed larger. It was what made retirement an increasingly attractive option. With a slight nod of the head, Robertshaw walked over to join his colleague at the car. Canham was watching him uneasily.

'I was out of order, Sarge,' he said. 'You're right, we have got a job to do.'

'No, lad, you're the one who's right. Nothing is worth that. Let's get out of here.'

'Good man,' said Canham, his relief showing. 'I mean, we can always argue that the inspector told us to go careful. It was the last thing he said at briefing, remember.'

'It was,' nodded Robertshaw, looking at his colleague over the top of the vehicle. 'Not that it feels right, mind. We've been treating this lot with kid gloves for too long.'

'Don't tell me,' said Canham, clambering into the driver's seat, 'tell the chief; it's his memo.'

Robertshaw gave a snort. All the officers at Abbey Road had read with disgust the chief constable's edict the week before that Western Division officers should treat The Spur with what he had described as 'extreme sensitivity'. The order had been issued following a series of late-night incidents in which the arrival on the estate of police officers had met with ferocious resistance and provoked disorder lasting several hours on one occasion. The incident that had prompted the memo had happened the week previously when a team of uniformed officers seeking to execute a warrant had smashed their way into a flat only to discover that they had the wrong address. The elderly lady who lived there had suffered a heart attack and had been in hospital ever since. It was not known if she would live.

The evening newspaper had seized on the story, suggesting that the police had caused the persistent violence by acting in a heavy-handed manner because, on two previous occasions, vans containing a dozen officers had arrived to make what should have been straightforward arrests. Ever sensitive to the media, the chief constable had sought to defuse the situation and had given an interview in which he revealed that he had instructed that all such future operations on The Spur be more carefully planned. His officers had hated the decision: the villains on The Spur had loved it and had lost no time in taunting the police whenever the opportunity arose. And, as every police officer knew, villains with a sense of invulnerability were dangerous animals indeed.

'Come on, get in, Bri,' said Canham from inside the car, reaching down to start the engine.

Robertshaw gave a final glance to his right, over to the entrance to the quadrangle where the blocks looped round to come within ten metres of each other and create a dark tunnel through which anyone wishing to leave the estate needed to travel. He lowered himself into the passenger seat and the car started to move. Robertshaw looked out of the passenger side window and saw figures running along one of the upper landings. More appeared at ground level in front of them, emerging from the shadows and starting to advance on the vehicle. Swivelling round to peer through the back window, he could see a small knot of people blocking off their escape route through the tunnel. Some appeared to be clutching baseball bats.

'Ambush,' hissed Robertshaw.

Canham slammed his foot on to the accelerator and swung the car round to face the tunnel before driving, with tyres screeching, towards the exit, scattering the assembled youths. As the car shot past, the officers heard a series of heavy thuds from the clubs slamming into its bodywork. With the gang's curses ringing in their ears but the way ahead clear, both officers nevertheless tensed as the vehicle approached the tunnel: not even the welcome sight of the street lights of the main road beyond could ease their concerns as the blocks of flats loomed large ahead of them, their sides steep and sheer like a canyon. Canham hit the accelerator hard, glancing in his rear-view mirror at the gang of men running across the square, their numbers swelling with every passing second as figures swarmed out of the darkness. Returning his attention to the way ahead, he saw another group appear from the shadows to their left and there was the sound of stones clattering off the side of the car. One cracked a window.

'Still want to stay?' said Canham, gripping tight on to the steering wheel.

'Just get us out of here.'

'Your wish,' said Canham and gunned the engine.

As the car plunged into the blackness of the tunnel, a metal dustbin plummeted from one of the upper floors and struck the ground just in front of the vehicle with a loud clang, its looming form briefly illuminated by the headlights as it bounced towards the car.

'Jesus!' yelled Canham, yanking on the steering wheel so that the car veered round the bin, scraping the vehicle's paintwork along the wall. The officers heard loud cheers from the mob behind them.

'That was close,' gasped Canham as the tunnel spat the car out of the far end.

Neither officer saw the concrete block falling silently through the air.

chapter two

'It gives me great pleasure to welcome you all this afternoon,' said the mayor, a balding man with a belly hardly contained by his red robes.

A smattering of applause rippled through the crowd of men, women and restless children crammed into the sweltering heat of the refurbished Tenby Street railway station. Those at the far end of the main platform, spilling out through the large double doors into the bright summer sunshine, strained to hear the mayor's words above the sound of the carnival that had been set up in the car park to celebrate the opening of the new railway museum. A fairground organ competed with the mayor for their attention.

'It has special significance for me,' continued the mayor, 'because I was myself a train driver.'

'I'm surprised he was able to fit into a cab,' murmured Detective Chief Inspector John Blizzard, who was standing at the front of the crowd. He glanced at his girlfriend and winked.

'Behave,' said Fee Ellis, pinching his arm.

'It gives me great personal pleasure to see so many young people here,' said the mayor, giving the children what he assumed to be a reassuring smile. 'It is so important that our younger generation takes an interest in Hafton's railway heritage. Before I perform the opening ceremony, I would like to ask John Blizzard to say a few words. Don't worry, he's not here to arrest anyone.'

The councillor paused for laughter – he had even scribbled the word 'laughter' on the speech – but none came so, with a slightly sheepish look, he glanced back down at his notes.

'Chief Inspector Blizzard,' he said, 'as many of you may know, is part of the team responsible for the renovation of this truly wonderful machine.'

The councillor gestured behind him to the stretch of track that ran through the station, out through the double doors and round the edge of the museum's field. Everyone stared at the steam locomotive, steaming gently, her green livery and polished metal gleaming in the shafts of sunshine filtering through the skylights in the station roof. There was a ripple of applause and Blizzard nodded his appreciation: for weeks, he had been saying that this moment meant more than all his judges' commendations. No one at Abbey Road could remember having seen Blizzard so enthusiastic about anything. Even to those who had known him for years, his relentless cheeriness had proved a wearing experience and they had started wishing for the return of the grumpier version. You knew where you were with the grumpier version, they told each other.

Less than two hundred metres away, the young woman and her golden retriever left their home and walked to the end of the terraced street. Following their daily ritual, they turned left at the last house and walked out on to the brick-strewn wasteland. Megan Rees paused, struck as ever by the contrast as they left the neatly kept former railwaymen's houses and confronted the desolate scene before them. The council had demolished ten nineteenth-century back-to-back streets the year before to make way for a supermarket but there had been no sign of the development promised by the city fathers. With a little shake of the head, Megan Rees set off across the wasteland, broken glass crunching beneath her calf-length boots.

At the far side of the wasteland, owner and dog clambered up the grassy embankment and dropped down on to the old railway siding. Thirty years previously, the line had served the city's giant railway works, but the tracks had been removed after the plant closed down and for three decades the signal box had kept a silent vigil for locomotives that would never come. Over the years, the trackbed had returned to nature, and these days, the majority of people using it were dog walkers enjoying the solitude of the rough track as it wound its way unheralded past terraced streets and run-down factories, a welcome splash of greenery in the grey heart of the city.

Megan Rees liked being there and she reached down to release the catch on the dog's lead, smiling as she watched the animal rooting in among the rotting sleepers and rusting barrels. She turned her attention to the myriad of wildflowers that poked through the scrub and admired the butterflies flitting from bloom to bloom as the sun warmed the earth. Something about their colours appealed to the artistic side of her nature and she produced a small notepad from her rucksack. For a couple of minutes, she sketched one of the insects as it fluttered between the flowers. Work completed, she gave a little nod of satisfaction and slipped the pad back into her bag, resolving that it would be her next project at night class. She mouthed a silent 'thank you' as the butterfly passed close to her face, so near that she could almost reach out and touch it. The insect's ragged wings reminded Megan Rees that butterflies were brutal creatures when it came to their own: the thought appealed to something deep within her.

Taking notice for the first time of the hubbub coming from the carnival at the nearby railway museum, Megan peered to her right and glimpsed, a hundred metres away through the high wire fence and the belt of trees, people milling about in the grounds of the refurbished station. She resolved to pop along later. It sounded fun. Her father would have enjoyed it, she thought. A railman through and through, Denny Rees would have appreciated the way the city was finally acknowledging the legacy of a once-great industry. Too many people had ignored the city's railway heritage for too long, that's what he would have said, she thought. Her face clouded over: if only he had been there to see it. Megan instinctively wiped a hand across moist eyes, the memory of his death still hurting more than a decade later. There was also anger at the manner of his passing. It was an anger that never left her: if anything, it grew stronger with each passing year. It was what had sustained her during her long wait for this moment.

Thought of her father returned Megan's focus to what she had come to do. She walked over to the old signal box, took a deep breath and climbed the stairs, stepping carefully as the rotting timbers creaked and shifted beneath her feet. She wanted to savour the moment. At the top of the steps, she let her gaze roam around the control room. Time had not been kind to the box: its controls had long since been ripped out and sold for scrap metal, all its windows had been smashed and the walls were defaced with graffiti. But there was another thing that caught her attention, something she was expecting to see, and she walked over to the shape lying in the far corner, her boots reverberating on the wooden floor. She stared down at the body then tapped it with her foot.

'Hello, Billy,' she said quietly. 'Welcome home.'

Megan walked over to the window and stared down into the siding, giving a slight intake of breath as she saw a young couple walking below, hand in hand. The young man glanced up and saw Megan staring at him. For a moment, they looked at each other then he returned his attention to his girlfriend and the young couple walked on. At the end of the siding, the young man glanced back to see Megan Rees still watching him from her vantage point at the window. When the couple had gone, Megan fished her mobile phone out of her pocket and dialled 999.

Detective Sergeant David Colley sat in the CID room at Abbey Road police station and bleakly surveyed the reports piled high on the desk. As weekend duty sergeant, he had been hoping for a quiet Saturday to catch up on some work. Some hope, he thought darkly. Western Division did not do quiet Saturdays – did not do quiet anything – and the incident reports had arrived in a steady stream throughout the morning. Burglaries, car thefts, assaults, the daily fare of life in the division, piled up in front of him, provoking a growing sense of helplessness in the sergeant.

Suddenly weary, Colley tipped his chair backwards and placed his feet on the desk, moving aside some of the files to make room. His eyes flickered then closed: ever since the birth of his baby daughter some weeks before, the sergeant had been experiencing a fatigue he had not thought possible. How he had scoffed when colleagues had tried to warn him in the weeks leading up to her arrival that he would feel more tired than he had ever known. 'I've done night shifts,' he had said with unaccustomed pomposity, 'I think I can handle a bit-babby.' Long nights endlessly pacing the floor with Laura in his arms, or sitting watching second-rate American cop shows at three in the morning, not daring to move lest he disturb his daughter as she slept on his lap, had made him realize the folly of those words.

He realized it again now as, slipping into slumber, he threatened to overbalance. Snapping open his eyes and giving a cry of alarm as he threw out a hand to steady himself against the wall, the sergeant gingerly lowered the chair back to the floor, sighed and reached out for a file. After a few moments, he cursed and hurled it back on to the desk, having read the same line four times without taking in any of the meaning. There was a knock on the door and in walked a slim, tall man with short-cropped brown hair, an angular face, a prominent nose and a thin mouth. Detective Inspector Chris Ramsey, smartly dressed as ever in a dark suit, glanced round the empty room.

'Where are the others?' he asked.

'Out on jobs. I sent Danny to the Castleview. I thought we ought to get something moving on the distraction burglaries ASAP – one of the victims is ninety-three and the newspaper has already been on to him. Turns out he's a war veteran. "I died at Dunkirk for the likes of them as robbed me" that kind of thing. Thought a swift response might make for a bit of good PR.'

'Indeed,' nodded Ramsey approvingly. 'Although most of the paper's time seems to be taken up with what happened on The Spur.'

'Any word?'

'I have just been in with the uniform inspector,' said Ramsey, easing himself into a chair. 'She's furious.'

'The concrete block landed on the bonnet, didn't it?'

'Yeah, but it flipped off to one side. It doesn't bear thinking about what would have happened if it had kept going.'

'Gazza still in hospital?'

'Yeah,' said Ramsey. 'Turns out that he fractured his shoulder trying to control the car – God knows how he managed to drive back to the station. He must have been in agony.'

'He would have been. I did that playing rugby. How's Bri?'

'Cuts and bruises but he's really shaken up. Some of the lads reckon he might put in for early retirement.'

'Surely he's seen it all before?'

'The lads reckon he's hacked off that uniform did not pile in there and sort it out straight away.'

'How come they didn't?'

'You read the memo,' said Ramsey.

'Crazy,' said Colley with a shake of the head. 'I mean, we could have lost an officer there last night. *Another* officer.'

There was silence for a moment.

'However,' said Ramsey, keen to change the subject, 'For the moment, the high-ups are still working out how to play it so it's not a CID job. Yet.'

'I suppose we should be thankful for small mercies,' said Colley, glancing at the files on his desk. He noticed the piece of paper in the inspector's hand. 'That's not another job, I hope.'

'We've got a body, I'm afraid. I'd go myself but I've got to do interviews with those lads we brought in for the Kingston Avenue job. Sorry.'

'Where was it found?' sighed the sergeant.

'Tenby Street.'

'Not the new railway museum?' asked Colley, reaching out for the piece of paper.

'Very close, apparently. Blizzard's over there, isn't he?'

'One of the guests of honour. Surely you've heard him banging on about it. It's been like working with Fred bloody Dibnah.' Colley glanced down at the paper. 'Who's this Megan Rees, then?'

'Found the body. Uniform are hanging on to her until you arrive. Keep it low key, eh? Don't want to disrupt the opening ceremony unless we really have to. Mind, there's so many people there, I can't see any way that folks will not cotton on that something has happened.'

'I think you can safely say,' said Colley as he eased himself to his feet and took his suit jacket down from a peg on the wall, 'that Blizzard is going to love this – absolutely bloody love it.'

With a sour look on his face, the sergeant walked out into the corridor. Heading towards him was Brian Robertshaw, his battered face bearing the marks of the incident the night before.

'Bri,' said Colley with genuine concern, 'how are you?'

'I got lucky. Gary is a real mess.'

'How come you're not at home?'

'The inspector wanted to run through what happened: the top brass are still making up their minds about what to do.' Robertshaw's voice assumed an edge. 'I mean, how much more do they want to know before we sort the bloody place out?'

'Word is you are thinking of quitting over it.'

'I've been in tight spots before, Dave,' said Robertshaw, anger replaced by bewilderment, 'but last night, last night was different.'

'How so?'

'Last night,' said Robertshaw quietly, 'I thought I was going to die. I tell you, Davy lad, nothing's worth throwing your life away like that. Nothing on earth. I've got a couple of kids and I want to see them grow up.'

Images of his baby daughter flashing into his mind, Colley nodded.

'And,' continued Robertshaw, limping down the corridor, 'if the top brass are not prepared to back us when this kind of thing happens, what is the point? I mean, I ask you, Davy lad, what is the point?'

As the mayor droned on, Blizzard let his gaze roam round the bright and airy museum, remembering how the building had looked when he started his campaign to save the station from the bulldozers. Long since closed, the station had fallen into dereliction, dark and scorched by arsonists' flames, its windows smashed by vandals, the building deemed a danger to public safety and earmarked for demolition by Hafton City Council. Blizzard and fellow members of the city's railway appreciation society had thought differently, protesting that the nineteenth-century station building was too valuable to lose, that it was one of the oldest railway stations in northern England. It would make, they had said in meetings with council officers, the ideal home for the Silver Flyer, the steam locomotive that the society had been restoring for several years. Blizzard's gaze settled on the nearby council dignitaries and he scowled. The inspector recalled how some of them had tried to block the plan, arguing that the money could be better spent elsewhere.

Looking to his left, Blizzard saw a tall, grey-haired man with bushy eyebrows and bony, almost gaunt, features, the eyes slightly hooded. The inspector smiled broadly. It was only when former railman Steve McGarrity contacted friends on the city council, themselves retired rail workers, that the campaign to save the station had proved successful. Recalling the moment his friend told him that a combination of grants would allow the museum to be created, the inspector grinned. McGarrity glanced across at the inspector, noticed the grin, gestured towards the mayor and faked a yawn. Blizzard chuckled and glanced at Fee.

'Alright?' she whispered.

'I can't remember when I've been happier,' beamed Blizzard. 'I can't think of a single thing that could ruin today.'

'Soft get,' she said and gave his arm a squeeze.

chapter three

After viewing the body, David Colley clumped down the signal box steps and into the mid-afternoon sunshine. For a few moments, he stood and watched the uniformed officers talking to an attractive young redhead on the top of the embankment. Colley had always liked redheads and, without realizing he had done it, found himself admiring the shapely form of Megan Rees in her tight blue T-shirt, faded jeans and the gleaming oxblood boots. Very nice, he thought, very nice. Reminded him of Jay when he first met her. She had been in her early twenties as well. Thought of his live-in girlfriend prompted an uneasy feeling of guilt. He knew why he was thinking like this: since the birth of their baby, there had not been much … Noticing Megan Rees watching him out of the corner of her eye, the faintest hint of a smile on her lightly freckled face, Colley rebuked himself for the lapse and tried to assume a more professional manner.

'Miss Rees,' he said, clambering up the embankment, 'I am Detective Sergeant Dave Colley. I understand you found the body?'

She nodded at her dog, which was now exploring the far side of the siding.

'Rocky found it.'

'How come he was in there?'

'I imagine he was chasing a rabbit,' said Megan. 'That's what he usually does.'

'All the way up there?' asked the sergeant doubtfully, gesturing to the signal box. 'Exactly what kind of rabbit are we talking about here, Miss Rees?'

'He gets excited.'

Was it the sergeant's imagination or was there a twinkle in her eyes as she said it?

'So, it gives me great pleasure to announce,' said the mayor, looking lovingly at the locomotive, 'that the Silver Flyer will be a permanent exhibit here. It will be a fitting home for her. It seems appropriate that, on this important occasion, Chief Inspector Blizzard tells you a little bit about how the Silver Flyer was saved from the scrapheap.'

All eyes turned to the inspector as he walked to the front. Aged in his late forties, a broad-chested man slightly heavier than someone of five feet ten inches should be, he was wearing his usual dark suit. Ceremony or not, his red tie dangled loosely at its customary half-mast position. Reaching the lectern, he produced a crumpled piece of paper from his suit jacket pocket. A man who had long relied on instinct when it came to addressing police briefings, the inspector had nevertheless felt compelled to rehearse this speech time and time again, standing in front of the bedroom mirror trying to ignore his paunch and the way that his tousled brown hair was greying at the temples. Now the moment had come, he surveyed the expectant faces of the audience, glanced down at his notes and took a deep breath.

'Thank you, Mr Mayor,' he said. 'Looking at the Old Lady today reminds me of the day I found her. She was in a terrible state. I can remember thinking what a shame it would be if ...'

*

The three officers stood on the top of the embankment and watched Megan Rees make her way across the wasteland, the dog close at her heels.

'I reckon she likes our sergeant here,' said one of the uniforms, winking at the other constable, he added. 'Just your type as well, Davey lad.'

Colley gave him a sour look but, before he could reply, the sergeant's attention was distracted by loud crackling from the direction of the nearby railway museum and the sound of a man bellowing something that none of the officers could quite make out. There was a smattering of applause. After the whine of guitar feedback shrieking through an amplifier, the man started singing raucously:

Everybody's doin' a brand new dance now
(C'mon baby do the loco-motion)
I know you'll get to like it
If you give it a chance now
(C'mon baby do the loco-motion).

'Forget chummy,' winced one of the uniforms. 'Someone should arrest that bloke for murdering a good song.'

'Aye,' said Colley, 'Blizzard will love that.'

To the others' amusement, the sergeant mimicked the dour tones of the chief inspector.

'Bloody pop band, what were they thinking of, David? No respect for the city's railway heritage. Do you know how many worple sprockets we used in the Old Lady? Seven million – seven sodding million, that's how many.'

The constables laughed.

'Hey,' said the sergeant, glancing hopefully at them, 'I

don't suppose either of you fancy nipping over to tell him that we—?'

His voice tailed off as their looks said it all.

Five minutes later, as Blizzard completed his speech and the applause broke out again, the inspector gave a huge sigh of relief and returned to another squeeze of the arm from Fee Ellis.

'Was that OK?' whispered the inspector.

'Very good.'

Blizzard looked across at Steve McGarrity who gave him a thumbs-up before returning his attention to the mayor.

'Thank you, Chief Inspector,' said the mayor with a smile. 'A most *arresting* talk, I think you will all agree.'

Again, he paused for laughter that did not come.

'Yes, well,' he continued quickly, moving over to a small blue curtain on the wall and reaching for the draw-string. 'It is now my very great pleasure to formally declare open this fine new museum and to reveal the name selected.'

He pulled the cord and the curtain swished open to reveal a plaque bearing the words *In Steam*.

'What kind of name's that?' snorted Blizzard as people started to clap.

'Will you behave,' hissed Fee, noticing the looks from several city councillors.

Blizzard continued to grumble as, ceremony at an end, the crowd started to drift away. The inspector's demeanour changed when he spotted a willowy redhead wave at them then start to work her way through the throng. Blizzard beamed when he saw the baby fast asleep in the pouch swung around her front: it was the same every time the inspector saw his god-daughter.

'How does she do it?' whispered Fee.

'Do what?' asked Blizzard.

'She only had the baby nine weeks ago and look at her, it's like it never happened.'

'You're not exactly a porker yourself,' said the inspector.

'Is that supposed to be a compliment?'

He nodded reassuringly.

'Do you know,' said Fee, 'I have been out with men who said the wrong thing at the right time, the right thing at the wrong time but very rarely with a man who managed to do both at the wrong time.'

'What did I say?'

The arrival of Jay and baby Laura brought the discussion to an end.

'And what have you done with my boyfriend?' asked Jay accusingly, fixing Blizzard with a stern look. 'Making the poor man work on a lovely summer's day like this?'

'Yeah,' muttered Blizzard, 'I'm sorry about that but I did say—'

'I think,' said Fee as Jay winked at her, 'that she is pulling your pud.'

'Don't worry, I know how it works,' said Jay, gently resting her hand on his arm for a moment.

Blizzard was about to reply when he noticed Steve McGarrity edging through the crowds towards them.

'Sorry to interrupt, ladies,' he said with a gentlemanly nod, 'but would it be possible to have a couple of moments of John's time?'

'We'll go and get an ice cream,' said Fee and the women wandered off to explore the carnival.

'Congratulations on the speech,' said McGarrity. 'Better than the mayor's piss-poor attempt. The man's always been a buffoon. I always reckoned it was a miracle that he managed to point the bloody engine in the right direction.'

'I suppose he did his best,' said Blizzard then noticed a

figure working its way slowly through the crowd towards them. 'Tommy's really struggling, isn't he?'

McGarrity followed his gaze towards the heavy-set, jowly man in his early sixties, who wore an ill-fitting hired black suit and whose lank black hair was slicked down with gel for the big occasion. Every step seemed to be an effort and even from this distance they could hear Tommy Rafferty's wheezing chest.

'Never seen him this bad,' nodded McGarrity.

Breathing heavily, Rafferty walked up to them and extended a hand to each of them in turn. Blizzard tried to ignore how clammy his grip felt.

'Museum's looking good,' said Rafferty.

'Yeah, but I'm not sure about the name,' said Blizzard. 'In bloody Steam, what's that about, Steve? I mean, a nine-year-old could have done better. Who chose it, for God's sake?'

'A nine-year-old. In a wheelchair.'

He glanced over at the young girl, who was having her photograph taken by a press photographer.

'Ah,' said Blizzard and looked uncomfortable before brightening up as he noticed people flocking round the Silver Flyer. 'Still, no matter, eh? I mean, this is about celebrating the romance of—'

There was gentle tap on the inspector's shoulder and he turned to look into the face of David Colley.

'Sorry, guv,' said the sergeant.

Blizzard's smile faded.

chapter four

'**W**ell whoever he was,' said Blizzard, staring down at the body as the sound of the fairground organ drifted across from the nearby railway museum, 'he certainly knew how to ruin a party.'

Colley nodded as he and the chief inspector stood in the signal box and surveyed the dead man. With a sigh, Blizzard walked over to the shattered window and gloomily stared down at the two uniformed officers taping off the far end of the siding. His gaze slid over to the station, vaguely glimpsed through the belt of trees.

'Might have known something like this would happen,' he sighed. 'I just hope no one spots our lads.'

'I asked them to be low-key about it. Mind, there's a limit to how long we can keep something like this quiet. We've already had two or three people sticking their neb in.'

'I'll bet you have.' Blizzard looked back at the body. 'It would help if we knew who he was.'

'The lads were wondering if we should call him the Railway Man,' suggested Colley with a mischievous smile. 'In keeping with the theme of the day.'

Blizzard said nothing and continued to gaze moodily out of the window. As the silence lengthened, Colley left him to his contemplation and tried instead to read the clues presented by the corpse. It was something Blizzard had taught him when they first started working together. *'Let the dead speak to you,'* the DCI was fond of declaring: one of his favourite sayings. One of many, it had to be said, thought Colley as he crouched down by the corpse. And what was this man saying? Surveying his wiry frame, the thinning black hair and straggly beard flecked with grey and the metal-rimmed spectacles, the sergeant decided that he was in his mid fifties, maybe even sixty. The weatherbeaten and lined face indicated a man who had lived an outdoor life, an impression confirmed by the hoary state of his hands, gnarled and pitted with the passing years. The hands of a manual worker, perhaps a railman come back to relive some old memories, Colley thought as the fairground music continued to hang in the afternoon air.

But no, decided the sergeant, crouching lower to obtain a better view of the body, this man was more than that. Much more. His hands told a different story: two of the knuckles looked as if they had been broken long ago and had healed badly. Or been broken again, perhaps. Manual worker possibly, but had this man, the sergeant asked himself, also been someone who lived by the code of violence? And perished by it? He would not be the first in Hafton, thought Colley as he straightened up. The sergeant had seen many such injuries over the years among those who had forged their reputations on the streets of the city, hard men thrown up from the ranks of the railmen, the shipyard workers and the stevedores who spent their pay packets on ale and brawled their way through a Friday night.

Without realizing he had done it, the sergeant flexed his right wrist where it had been fractured by one such drunken brawler during his early days as a uniformed officer. Then a rookie uniformed constable, Colley had stepped in to break up two youths fighting outside one of the city-centre clubs. It was as he was sitting in A and E waiting to be treated later that night that Colley had learned a valuable lesson: it had been Brian Robertshaw who told him that the way to deal with such incidents was to let the drunks knock seven shades out of each other before the uniforms intervened. Safer that way, Robertshaw had said. Thought of Robertshaw took the sergeant's mind over to events at The Spur the night before and he frowned. Robertshaw had been right: everyone knew the estate's reputation but this had been different. Outside the rules of the game by which everyone played.

The sergeant was about to walk over to join Blizzard at the window when something caught his eye and he peered closer at the dead man: although the hair was black, there were several brown strands poking through. Puzzled, the sergeant straightened up and walked over to the window where the two detectives peered through the trees at the crowds milling around the renovated station building. Colley was about to say something when they heard a man's indistinct voice as he struggled against the crackling second-rate PA system, his voice fading away then returning in sudden booms as the man attempted in vain to be heard over the noise of the fairground organ.

'Didn't know they'd booked Norman Collier,' said Colley.

Blizzard chuckled.

'Mind,' added the sergeant, with a sly look at the inspector, 'he would have been better than the sentimental shite you trotted out in your speech. Did I hear correctly that you banged on about romance again?'

Blizzard stared uncertainly at his sergeant for a few moments then recognized the impish look and smiled. Few at Abbey Road could get away with such humour at the chief inspector's expense, certainly not concerning something which he held so dear. The quip lifted the sombre atmosphere in the sweltering signal box.

'No respect, young David,' said Blizzard as he crossed the room and crouched down by the body. 'So, go on, who do we have here?'

Colley paused. Wait for it, he thought, wait for it.

'Is he talking to you?' asked Blizzard.

'He certainly is. He's saying someone gave him a right howking and would I nick the bastard who did it?'

Blizzard surveyed the way the man's right leg was twisted grotesquely beneath the body, the ankle protruding at an unnatural angle. Ignoring the sickening sight of the bone poking through the skin, he glanced at the ripped shirt, one sleeve almost hanging off, and at the jeans, the long smears of dried mud and torn knees suggesting the victim had been dragged across the stony ground outside.

'He didn't give up without a fight,' said the inspector.

'I suspect that's how he lived his life, guv.'

'He tell you that?'

Colley nodded and the inspector shot him an approving look. Blizzard let his gaze stray up to the man's face. He surveyed the caked blood that had welled from the ugly wound on the forehead, matting the straggly beard then trickled down his cheeks, staining the man's smashed teeth. He looked at the misshapen and swollen nose and the numerous gashes that partially obscured the man's features.

'Some of these injuries are certainly old,' said Blizzard. 'He's had that busted nose a long time. You reckon he was a scrapper?'

'Yeah. Look at his hands. This man has been through the mill plenty of times.'

'Well he lost this time,' said the inspector as he straightened up, grimacing when his right knee cracked. 'This is as bad a beating as I've seen. Have you noticed his hair?'

'I'm wondering if it's dyed.'

'For why?'

'Vanity. Or maybe because he did not want to be recognized. Our Railway Man is a bit of a mystery, all things considered.'

'He is indeed,' said the inspector and looked back to the dead man: there was something he could not quite place. It kept nagging away at the back of his mind. 'I keep thinking I should know his name.'

'He a villain then?'

Racking his memory, the inspector tried to summon up the name from somewhere. Eventually, he shook his head.

'No use,' he said. 'Who found him?'

'Dog-walker.'

'Isn't it always?' said Blizzard as the two men made their way carefully down the rotting stairs and out into the bright afternoon sunshine. 'When I retire, I'm going to go to university and do a thesis on what breed of dog is most likely to find a corpse.'

'Hafton would probably give you a grant for it. My niece is going there to do media studies, whatever that is.'

Blizzard snorted and was about to say something when there came the sound which never failed to send a tingle down his spine, the long drawn-out whistle of the Silver Flyer.

'Took us ages to find that whistle,' said the inspector proudly, 'Bobby Ford found it in a scrapyard in Doncaster in the end. Picked it up for a tenner. I mean, can you believe that? A tenner. Must be worth three or four hundred. And the lads reckon that some of the name plates could be worth the same to a collector. It's a real delight to see her steaming again and—'

His voice tailed off as he noticed the sergeant's smile.

'What?' he said.

'You, guv. Just you.'

Blizzard gave him a rueful look but his face clouded over as he saw the plume of steam billowing into the air as the Silver Flyer began its first trip round the grounds, pulling a carriage full of excited families.

'This really is the last thing we want, David,' he said. 'On a day like this. It'll ruin everything.'

'Tell me about it. I've got a mountain of work on, as it is. We had sixteen burglaries last night and the DI's tied up with that supermarket job over in Kingston Avenue. That's another bloody bath-time missed.'

Blizzard looked at his colleague. Sudden flashes of irritation had been one of the things the chief inspector had noticed about Colley since the birth of baby Laura. There had been tell-tale signs in his appearance as well. Tall and lean, the sergeant was, as always, smartly turned out, his black hair neatly combed, his round, almost boyish, face clean-shaven and his dark blue shirt perfectly ironed, but the bags beneath the eyes told their own tale. So did the laboured way he moved, the sergeant's natural athleticism banished beneath an invisible weight.

'You OK?' asked Blizzard.

'Just a bit tired.'

'I can keep an eye on things if you want to take a flyer.'

'You know that's not the way it works, guv. Besides, haven't you got that railway association dinner?'

'I can skip it.'

Colley shook his head. 'I know how much it means to you. I'll be fine, honest. We've got plenty in if we need them.'

The inspector glanced along the old trackbed toward the plume of steam once more. Staring past the officers completing the taping off of the scene, he could just make out through the trees the occasional white head among the children slurping ice creams. Blizzard knew who they belonged to, a number of retired railmen from across the north who had attended today, some of whom had travelled from the old railway towns of Sheffield and Doncaster to be guests at the opening before attending the dinner being staged in the Railway Hotel that night.

'Maybe,' mused Blizzard, 'the dinner could be relevant to the inquiry.'

'You think chummy was a railman come back for the opening?'

'Be tragic if he was. They're the salt of the earth, those old railmen. They really are.'

The detectives heard a muttered curse and turned to watch, with some amusement, a dapper figure slip-sliding his way down the embankment. Having reached the bottom, Detective Inspector Graham Ross, divisional head of forensics at Abbey Road, wiped his shiny black shoes with a pale-blue handkerchief produced from his breast pocket. Job done, he picked his way carefully across the uneven ground, trying to prevent flecks of dried earth getting on to his trousers. Blizzard winked at his sergeant: everyone knew that Graham Ross prided himself on his appearance. Today was no different: his brown wavy hair was beautifully groomed, there was not a suspicion of stubble on his face and he was dressed immaculately, in a pressed grey designer suit with a blue silk tie.

'Ah, Versace,' said Blizzard affably. 'How nice of you to join us.'

'Can't you lot find bodies somewhere more convenient?' Ross looked irritably round the siding. 'So where is our little friend?'

'I'll show you,' said Blizzard, gesturing to the signal box. 'It's dirty up there, mind.'

'Isn't it always?' sighed Ross.

Having walked across to the box, the three officers

climbed gingerly up the creaking steps. Once at the top, the banter died away, to be replaced by a more sombre atmosphere as Blizzard pointed to the body in the corner of the control room.

'Any idea who he is?' asked Ross, glancing at the inspector.

'We wondered if he might be a former railman.'

Ross walked over to the corpse, crouched down and stared at the body.

'Well, you might just be right there,' he murmured.

'What did I say?' said Blizzard with a triumphant look at Colley. 'I said that he was a ... Hang on, how do you know that?'

Ross examined the brown strands of hair poking through the black then looked closely at the dead man's broken knuckles. The detective carefully lifted up the man's bloodstained shirt to reveal the outline of a poorly removed tattoo emblazoned across the chest.

'Because believe it or not,' he said, looking up at the detectives, 'I reckon this is Billy Guthrie.'

'I thought I knew him from somewhere,' said Blizzard, with a low whistle. 'But are you sure? He looks a lot different from his mug shots.'

'He does look different but he definitely had a tattoo like that and I reckon his hair's been dyed. And he didn't wear spectacles when I knew him.'

'We reckoned that this was a man who did not want to be recognized,' nodded Blizzard.

'Hardly surprising.'

'Is anyone going to tell me who Billy Guthrie was?' asked Colley.

'If you'd ever worked in Burniston, you wouldn't need to ask,' replied Ross.

'He a villain then?'

'*The* villain. Burniston's hard man. I came across him when I was a uniformed sergeant there; I tell you, Dave, I have not been scared of many people in my life but Billy Guthrie, Jesus.'

'A nutter then?'

'Yeah,' said Ross, 'but what made him all the more dangerous is that he was a boxer so he knew how to handle himself.'

'I told you he was a scrapper,' said the sergeant with satisfaction. 'He any good?'

'My dad always reckoned that he could have made something of himself if he had stuck at it.'

'Don't tell me he could have been a contender,' said Colley with a slight smile.

'Dad said he could have fought for the British title. His trainer was a bloke called Roly Turner and he's trained some good fighters in his time. Runs that club down the back of the Naafi.' Ross glanced at the inspector. 'Roly was a railman as well, guv. I guess that's how they met.'

'So was Guthrie really that good?' asked Colley.

'Oh, aye. I remember my dad telling me how he saw him fight for the Eastern Counties title at the Victoria Hall one night. Took him two minutes to win. They had to lift the other lad back over the ropes, he was in such a state.'

'So if he was that good, how did he end up here?' asked the sergeant, gesturing to the signal box.

'Usual story – used his fists too readily out of the ring. Pub brawls mostly. Not that we ever got anything to stick. Problem finding witnesses brave enough to speak out against him in court. Folks were terrified of Billy Guthrie. Not sure anybody minded when he vanished.'

'Vanished?' asked the sergeant.

'Yeah, must have been 10–12 years ago.' Ross looked at Blizzard for confirmation. 'Mid-eighties, I reckon.'

'About that,' nodded the inspector.

'Guthrie had been out of the fight game for a while but he tried a comeback against some kid, in the Victoria Hall again. It was a big story at the time: the local rag made a huge thing of it, special pull-out and the like.'

'I assume Guthrie lost?' said Colley.

'I don't think anyone won,' said Blizzard, walking over to stare out of the window. 'Guthrie head-butted the kid.'

'Injured him really badly,' nodded Ross. 'There was uproar. Damned near a riot in the hall, folks trying to get at Guthrie, the medics trying to look after the kid. Cops had to call in extra bodies to calm things down.'

'Come to think of it, I do remember something,' nodded Colley. 'I assume that our friend vanished after that?'

'Not quite – see, that was on the Saturday, then the following Wednesday, Guthrie turns up in the Queen's Head in Burniston. Starts kicking off. He was always kicking off when he'd had a few sherbets, was Billy. Picked on some Hafton lads. The landlord tried to stop him and got a smack for his troubles. The poor bloke was in a coma for fourteen months before he died.'

'That's where I knew about it from,' said Blizzard. 'Because the lads Guthrie picked the fight with were from our patch, Burniston asked us to take a statement but they all kept stuum. Then, like Graham says, Guthrie simply dropped off the face of the planet.'

'Without so much as a by-your-leave,' nodded Ross. 'Him and his wife and their teenage daughter. No one knew where they had gone, or if they did, they weren't telling. The house stood empty for the best part of a year then the building society repossessed it.'

'So, did no one see Guthrie at all after that?' asked Colley.

'That's the weird thing, Dave. We circulated his details to other forces but it all came to nothing. Mind, if he had changed his appearance that would explain a lot. He did have a lot to hide from. The Rees family were livid – said he had gotten away with murder.'

'Rees?' said Colley sharply.

'Yeah, the dead pub landlord was called Denny Rees. Why?'

'The girl who found him is called Megan Rees.'

'Sounds like you've got someone with a motive then,' said Ross. 'She's the daughter.'

'I'll bring her in,' said the sergeant, disappearing down the stairs.

When he had gone, Blizzard returned his attention to the corpse.

'So how come chummy is here, Graham?' he asked. 'If we assume he left the area because people were looking for him, what brought him back?'

The Old Lady's whistle pierced the afternoon air again.

'Perhaps *she did*,' said Blizzard. 'You said he worked on the railways. What if he was making a sentimental journey to see the Old Lady?'

'I'm not sure Billy Guthrie did sentiment.'

Blizzard looked down at the dead man's battered features.

'No,' he said, 'I don't suppose he did.'

chapter five

Fee Ellis was waiting outside the museum when Blizzard pushed his way through the crowds ten minutes later, the inspector wrinkling his nose in distaste at the sound coming from the band performing in the marquee. He smiled when he saw the detective constable standing on the steps. Five feet eight and slim with short, slightly waved, blonde hair and wearing dark trousers and a grey T-shirt, she was, at twenty-eight, nearly two decades his junior. They had been together for a couple of years and he was starting to believe that it may be the real thing. Fee had been a police officer for eight years. Having graduated from university, she had served as a uniformed constable for five years, over on the east side of the city before being moved to Western Division CID. The daughter of a retired detective sergeant, with whom Blizzard had worked briefly in his early days, Fee had impressed the chief inspector the moment she had walked into the squad room, and not just for her undoubted abilities as a detective. However, having gone through an acrimonious divorce as a young man, it had taken a long time for Blizzard to ask her out. Now, as ever when they were working together, Blizzard assumed a professional air.

'What we got?' he asked as the officers walked into the building and through what had once been the main ticket office but which was now a gift shop.

'Not much yet. We've kept it low-key like you said.'

'Yeah, don't want to panic folks,' said Blizzard, pausing to examine one of the railway books on a shelf. 'I might come back and buy that. Thought it was out of print.'

'Trouble is,' said Fee as they began walking again, 'there are so many people moving about, it's going to be impossible to keep a track of everyone.'

'I appreciate that but there has got to be a chance that someone in there knows more than they are letting on.'

'Because of Guthrie's links with the railway?'

'Yeah,' said the inspector as they walked through a corridor lined with black-and-white photographs of steam locomotives, 'because of his links with the railways.'

They walked on to the main platform and the inspector surveyed the happy throng of families walking round the displays. One of the most popular attractions was the model railway that stretched for twenty-five feet along one wall of the museum. Children peered excitedly through the glass cover at the re-creations of the nineteenth-century Hafton line as it wound its way up from the docks and westwards through the city's outskirts before emerging out into rural flatlands dotted with villages. Blizzard himself had examined the model earlier in the day and had felt like a small boy again when he spotted the village where he lived.

There were plenty of larger exhibits as well and strolling around the locomotives and rolling stock had brought back memories of standing at the bottom of the garden when he was a child in Lincolnshire and waiting for the mighty steam locomotives to thunder past, the drivers waving back at him and sometimes, if he was lucky, letting rip with the whistle. Such memories were precious to John Blizzard and, watching the happy throng now, he felt a sudden rush of anger that someone should have ruined the day.

The inspector left Fee and another detective constable to

make discreet inquiries and walked over to where Steve McGarrity and Tommy Rafferty were standing, partially hidden by a large display case containing an old railway station bell. They were talking to a slim, earnest young man wearing green cords and a brown leather jacket. That it seemed to be a serious conversation did not surprise the inspector. Malcolm Watt was a serious man. Blizzard had known him for a number of years, beginning in the days when he was one of the city council's tourism officers and the first person to give credence to the idea of a railway museum. Ever mindful of his position as a council employee, Watt had nevertheless played an astute game of politics, linking up with McGarrity to convince some of the leading councillors that the concept was worth exploring further, always keeping Blizzard informed of developments. The inspector and Watt had developed a respect for each other and Blizzard had been delighted when it was announced that his new friend was to be the museum's manager.

'John, what the hell is happening?' hissed Watt as the inspector joined them. 'I've had half the councillors in the city asking me what your lot are doing in the siding.'

'I know, but—'

'And your officers have been asking people questions. Hardly makes for the best impression on a day like this, John. I mean, surely it could wait until tomorrow?'

'It's not my fault someone's been murdered,' said Blizzard defensively.

'Murdered?' gasped Watt.

'Keep your voice down,' said Blizzard quickly as people turned to look at them. 'My aim is to make sure that today passes off with the minimum of fuss but yes, we've found a body over in the signal box.'

'You'll not keep that quiet for long,' said McGarrity.

'Yeah, they've already been sniffing around,' said Watt,

nodding at a television crew interviewing the mayor in front of one of the locomotives. 'One of them nipped out for a fag and noticed your lot putting the tape up in the siding.'

'This body,' said McGarrity. 'Man or woman?'

'Man,' said Blizzard. 'Look, I shouldn't be telling you this but there's a reason we're asking questions here. We're pretty sure he's a former railman. Wondered if anyone might know him.'

'Who is he?' asked McGarrity.

'Bloke called Billy Guthrie.'

McGarrity gave a low whistle.

'You knew him?' asked Blizzard.

'Everyone knew Billy Guthrie,' and McGarrity glanced at Rafferty. 'You remember him, Tommy?'

'Nasty bit of work,' nodded Rafferty.

'Well, I need to track down his relatives. Someone has to ID the body.'

'Sorry,' said McGarrity, 'didn't know him that well, John.'

Blizzard looked at Rafferty, who shook his head firmly and turned away from the conversation. The inspector was struck by the thought that, even in death, it was always the same with Billy Guthrie. No one dared be associated with him when it came to police investigations. The irony was not lost on the chief inspector.

'Yes,' he began, 'but he can't hurt anyone now.'

'Sorry,' shrugged McGarrity, 'just didn't know him that well. I heard he left the city.'

'Look, John,' said Watt, 'I know you've got a job to do but I really must object about the way—'

'Like it or not,' said Blizzard as Fee walked over and stood waiting for the outcome of the conversation, 'my officers are going to have to keep asking questions. They can do it with your co-operation or without.'

'Do they have to? I mean why question people here? The

signal box is outside our perimeter fence. Nothing to do with us.'

'You never know in these situations.' Blizzard looked genuinely apologetic. 'Look, I'm really sorry about this, Malcolm, this is the last thing any of us wanted.'

With a scowl, the museum manager disappeared towards his office. Blizzard crossed to join Fee.

'Let's get out of here,' said Rafferty, glancing at McGarrity. 'We don't want Blizzard's lot asking us questions.'

Making sure that the detectives had not seen them, they slipped away through the crowds.

'Perhaps, Miss Rees,' said Colley, staring across the table in the stuffy little interview room, 'you can explain why you, of all the people, should be the one to discover the body of Billy Guthrie?'

Megan Rees returned his gaze for a few moments, allowing the sergeant to peruse her a little further. Colley had to admit it, he found her fascinating. However, the more he stared at her, the more he realized that the fascination was not so much about her attractive appearance but more about her demeanour. There was, concluded the sergeant, something strangely composed about her, a calmness at the centre of the storm and a sense that she knew things that no one else knew. Colley glanced across at the chief inspector sitting next to him. More accustomed to suspects breaking down under questioning, both officers had found themselves disconcerted by Megan Rees from the moment the interview had started twenty minutes previously.

Even on the drive to Abbey Road Police Station earlier that afternoon, Megan had said nothing, sitting in the back of the car and staring wordlessly out of the window, ignoring the uniformed officer sitting next to her and rebuffing Colley's attempts at conversation as he drove. Since arriving at the station, her silence had continued and now Colley sought some kind of steer from Blizzard, who was sitting with his arms folded. The inspector shrugged: the officers had agreed that since Megan had appeared to like the sergeant when they met in the railway siding, it made sense that he should lead on the interview. It was an approach that was getting them nowhere.

'Miss Rees,' said the sergeant more insistently, 'you really do have to co-operate with us.'

'Is someone looking after my dog?' She sounded worried.

The question startled the sergeant: it was the first time either detective had seen or heard her exhibit any emotion.

'Why do you ask?' he said.

'If you keep me in overnight, someone will need to make sure he is fed and walked.'

'Why should we keep you in overnight?'

'Don't look like that, Sergeant,' she said, the faintest of smiles playing on her face. 'It's not a *clue*. It's not a veiled admission that I killed Billy Guthrie.'

'I could understand if it was,' said the sergeant, nodding at Blizzard. 'I mean, we both know what you have been through.'

'Are you a father, Sergeant?'

Surprised by the question, Colley nodded.

'Yes. Just. A daughter.'

'Can you imagine what it would be like for her growing up without you?' asked Megan, fixing him with a stare. 'I mean, don't give me some mindless platitude, can you *really* imagine what it would be like for her if you were suddenly taken away from her?'

Without realizing he had done it, Colley shook his head and suddenly realized what it was about Megan Rees that so disturbed him: it was as if she had seen deep into his mind and discovered the secret fears that had crowded in

45

ever since he had first held his daughter in his arms. Fears he had not been expecting, fears that he felt acutely now every time he watched baby Laura sleeping. Frightening thoughts of having something so precious that nothing else in life seemed to matter. A fear that a criminal might flash a blade, pull a gun, and leave Jay and their daughter to fend for themselves in a hostile world. Such thoughts, never far from the sergeant's mind in recent weeks, had become more insistent in the hours since he had talked to Brian Robertshaw about events on The Spur. Sensing both Megan Rees and Blizzard watching him intently, Colley shook his head again.

'No,' he said quietly, detective's instincts returning as he realized that her comment might give him a way to move the interview forward. 'No, I can't imagine what it would be like for my daughter to live without me. Why do you ask?'

'I don't have to imagine. It's what I have had to do every second of the day,' said Megan, her voice infused with sudden anger. 'There is not a day, not a minute, that I do not think of my father.'

'Yes, I know and—'

'And if you ask me if I am glad that Billy Guthrie is dead, then the answer is yes, Sergeant.' Her eyes flashed fire. 'The answer is yes. Yes, I am glad that he is dead and, yes, I hope his death was slow and, yes, I hope that it was exceedingly painful.'

'Your anger is understandable. I know what happened that night your father was—'

'You know nothing,' she said, spitting the words out and startling the detectives with her venom. 'What did your lot do? What did anyone do? Nothing, that's what.'

'I am sure the investigating—'

'Don't defend them! When the police turned up at the pub, no one would even talk to them. No one had seen anything, apparently. Like it never happened. Like my father had never existed. Cowards, the lot of them. And your lot – your lot let him get away with it.' Her voice dropped. 'But I saw what happened. Oh, yes, I saw what happened.'

'You did?' said Blizzard, sitting forward in his seat and speaking for the first time in several minutes.

She nodded. 'All of it.'

'Then how come you never said anything to officers at the time?'

'My mother told me not to.'

'Why on earth would she say that?' asked Blizzard.

'She said Guthrie would only cause more trouble for us.' Her lip curled in anger. 'Can you believe that, your own mother telling you to do that? And what extra trouble could he cause? He had already taken away the most precious person of all.'

'Yet you still kept quiet,' said the inspector, 'despite all the things you have just said about the other witnesses, you said nothing.'

'I was eleven years old,' replied Megan and her face briefly assumed an expression of helplessness. 'What did I know? I mean, my own mother.'

Her expression hardened.

'I'm glad the bitch is dead.'

'And how did your mother die, Megan?' asked Blizzard softly.

'I know what you're thinking,' she said with another faint smile, back in control of her emotions, 'but I hate to disappoint you. I didn't kill her. She wasn't found with a big knife sticking out of her back with my name on the handle and a message, *Die, mummy dearest, do*. No, my mother died of a heart attack last year. Ironic really, since I'm not sure she even had a heart.'

The comment was delivered in a dispassionate manner

and Blizzard looked at her for a few moments, not sure how to take the young woman sitting defiantly before them, her arms crossed as if defying the detectives to challenge what she was saying. He glanced over at the sergeant, whose expression suggested that he, too, found the interview increasingly disturbing.

'Perhaps,' said Blizzard, 'it would help if you told us what you saw the night your father was attacked.'

'What good would it do now? Guthrie is dead; you can't touch him. Someone has already done that for you.'

'But it might help us work out who killed him.'

Megan shrugged.

'Please,' said Blizzard.

The intensity of his comment seemed to strike home and, after thinking for a few moments, she nodded.

'We lived over the pub,' she said. 'I had sneaked down because my mum said I could have a bottle of orange juice from the bar.'

The Queen's Head, a cavernous, former coaching house on the market place in Burniston, was virtually empty at nine o'clock that Wednesday evening. As Denny Rees stood behind the bar, polishing glasses, he perused those that had come in out of the rain. In one corner of the large wood-panelled lounge sat a small group of four middle-aged men enjoying a quiet pint. Rough, working men. Collecting the glasses earlier in the evening, he had heard them talking about a late-night poker game and surmised that they had travelled from Hafton to take part and were enjoying a few drinks beforehand.

Denny surveyed them with slight concern: Hafton may only be eleven miles to the south of Burniston but the city and the market town were worlds apart and everyone knew the two places did not mix. Denny had lost count of the trouble he had seen break out between men from the two communities. Having said that, these men seemed to be keeping themselves to themselves and the few locals seemed to be ignoring them. Indeed, the only other people in the pub were a young couple who only had eyes for each other as they sat by the window, and in one of the alcoves was one of his regulars, an old man nursing the pint he had bought an hour before. He wouldn't make much profit if they were all like that, thought Denny morosely. Because Wednesdays were never busy, Denny was working on his own. He could have brought in one of the barmaids but times were hard in Burniston and trade had been slow over previous weeks so he was doing anything he could to keep the costs down, keep the brewery happy.

Denny knew all about hard times. A former fitter, he had first been made redundant when the Hafton locomotive works closed in the mid sixties. Managing to find work once more, he had lost his job twice, first from a Hafton railway maintenance company in 1981 and again three years later when Burniston's largest engineering plant closed down. Eventually, with jobs scarce, he became the tenant at the Queen's Head, a job in which he excelled, quickly becoming popular with the regulars even though he had only been there six months.

Denny busied himself behind the bar. Surveying the four Hafton men out of the corner of his eye, he thought he vaguely recognized one of them, fancied that they might even have worked together on the shop floor at the locomotive works. Not that they had ever spoken: the works had employed six thousand people, after all. When the man had walked up to order more drinks, there had been a flicker of recognition but no words were spoken about their previous life. What Denny did remember was that the man was a decent sort, not the kind to kick off.

It was shortly after nine that the door to the pub swung open and in walked three men. Denny stiffened as he saw the leader, a burly man with a misshapen nose and a scar on his cheek. Billy Guthrie. The landlord knew all about Billy Guthrie. Trying to keep calm, Denny put down the glass he was polishing and watched silently as the arrivals walked up to the bar, all three of them casting ugly glances in the direction of the group in the corner.

'I thought I banned you, Billy,' said Denny calmly.

'Heard you were letting shite in so thought I would come and help you get rid of them.'

'I don't need help, and even if I did I would not ask for it from you.'

Guthrie's eyes flashed his anger.

'Besides,' said Denny, 'they can drink here if they like. It's a free country.'

Guthrie ignored the comment and walked towards the Hafton men, who eyed him nervously.

'Time to get out, lads,' said Guthrie.

'Stay where you are,' said Denny.

He reached beneath the bar and produced the truncheon which he had started keeping there since the night he had banned Guthrie for fighting. There had been plenty of rumours that Guthrie was looking for revenge and Denny Rees was not the kind of man to take any chances. Guthrie glared at Denny as he came round from behind the bar.

'In fact,' said Denny, 'it's time for you to get out, Billy. No one says who gets to drink in my pub but me. I barred you, remember.'

Guthrie eyed the truncheon for a few moments before walking up to Denny, until the two men were eyeballing each other. Denny could smell the drink on his breath. Guthrie looked past him and noticed Megan watching wide-eyed from behind the bar.

'I am sure that you would not want to do anything stupid in front of your daughter,' he said.

'You keep her our of this,' said Denny, half turning.

The punch was lightning quick, a hammer blow of a right fist smashing into the side of Denny's face. The force sent the landlord flying backwards. Everyone heard the sickening crack as his head struck the edge of the bar and he crashed to the floor.

'He did not move,' said Megan, her voice little more than a whisper. 'It may have taken him fourteen months to die but my father was dead from the moment he hit the floor. And if I hadn't been there, if he hadn't turned to ...'

Her voice tailed off and she started to sob. The two detectives had been sitting forward in their seats, listening in silence as she recounted her story. Now, as if a spell had been broken, Blizzard gave a little sigh, stood up and went to lean with his back against the wall. He closed his eyes for a moment: sometimes the raw human emotions he encountered in the job were too much to take. In a strange way he was relieved to feel the emotion knotted in his throat. It was somehow reassuring. The inspector had discussed the subject with Fee several times in recent weeks. Noting the way Colley had softened his response to some situations since the birth of the baby, Blizzard had found himself wondering why he felt no such inclination. Colley had always been the more compassionate one of the two officers but until the baby was born, Blizzard had not questioned his own reactions. Had not felt the need. Now, though, he found himself re-evaluating many things. Could it be, he had asked Fee, that you experienced so much heartbreak and evil that you eventually became too cynical, incapable of feeling genuine emotions, incapable even of loving? They had been in the local village pub at the time and Fee had nodded at his glass and suggested that it was the beer talking but the conversation had troubled them both.

Blizzard ran through the conversation now as he stood and watched Megan Rees, who sat at the table staring down at her clasped hands. And the inspector knew the answer: human pain was human pain and pain to be shared. He wondered if it was becoming a godparent that had done it. Responsibility of a different kind. This time it was Colley's turn to recognize his colleague's discomfort.

'You cannot blame yourself,' said the sergeant, looking across the table at Megan. 'You must never blame yourself for what happened.'

She gave a dry laugh after which there was silence in the interview room again. Blizzard returned to sit at the table.

'Megan,' he said, looking hard at her, 'time to level with us. If you had killed Billy Guthrie, people would understand. We would understand. Maybe you saw him in Hafton yesterday and lost it, maybe it was a crime of passion.'

'And how exactly did I lure him to the signal box?'

'You're an attractive young woman. Maybe you made him an offer that he could not refuse.'

'Isn't that called leading the witness?' The edge was back in the voice.

'I am just saying that you might have done anything to get back at him. A court might take the view that you attacked him when the balance of your mind was disturbed.'

'You're fishing, Chief Inspector.'

Damn, thought Blizzard, is it that obvious?

'Besides,' she continued, 'there is one major flaw in your argument. Surely you must have heard enough about Billy Guthrie to know that someone like me could never hope to do that. The man was a brute.'

'Yes, I app—'

'But it doesn't mean that I did not want to kill the bastard,' she said vehemently. 'Or have not done it every day in my dreams.'

Silence fell on the room: somehow there did not seem anything more to say. Twenty minutes later, the interview over, a pensive Colley was standing in the deserted CID room, clutching a mug of tea and staring out of the window at the summer storm clouds rolling in dark and heavy along the river. There had already been a couple of distant grumbles of thunder and the sergeant found himself perspiring in the suddenly heavy atmosphere. He turned when Blizzard walked in.

'Any more thoughts?' asked the inspector, sitting down at one of the desks and putting his feet up, grimacing as his bad knee protested again.

'She has such anger inside her. I mean, what is she – twenty three? – yet she feels like that.'

'You of all people should be able to understand.'

'Meaning?'

'The bond between father and daughter,' said the inspector. 'It's very strong. Laura may only be a few weeks old but I can already see the way she looks at you. The way she smiles.'

Colley considered the comment for a few moments then nodded.

'Becoming a father changes everything,' he said.

'So Fee keeps saying.'

'She still keen on the idea then?'

Blizzard nodded gloomily. Graham Ross walked in.

'How did it go with Megan Rees?' he asked.

'She reckons she saw Guthrie batter her father,' said Blizzard.

'That never came out in the original inquiry.'

'Reckons her mother told her to keep quiet.' Blizzard looked at the piece of paper in the DI's hand. 'What's that?'

'My preliminary report,' handing the document over and sitting down at one of the desks. 'It all points to the assault taking place in the railway siding. We are pretty sure it happened sometime after midnight.'

'How so sure?' asked Colley.

'The mud on his trousers. The ground was bone dry yesterday but the heavens opened at about midnight. The mud suggests he was out in it.'

'Weapon?' asked Blizzard.

'Not sure there was one. Looks like this was a good old-fashioned beating. Some beating, mind. And way beyond what Megan Rees could administer.'

'Maybe,' murmured Blizzard.

'Come on,' protested Ross. 'You surely cannot believe that a woman is capable of this. I mean, whoever did this used a tremendous amount of force and she's only a kid.'

'What do you think, David?' asked Blizzard, glancing over to his sergeant, who had resumed his vigil at the window.

'At the moment,' said the sergeant, without turning round, 'I'd believe anything of her.'

Silence fell on the room, which had suddenly darkened. There was another roll of thunder, much closer now, and the first drops of rain flecked against the glass, gently at first but within seconds driving much harder. A uniformed officer walked into the room, holding a copy of the evening newspaper.

'I think you'd better see this, sir,' he said.

'Have we run out of toilet roll?' asked Blizzard.

Colley and Ross exchanged amused glances: the inspector's disdain for the media was legendary. Dealing with journalists had always been the part of the job he liked least.

'I think you will want to see it,' said the uniformed constable. 'Spotted it when I was looking for an in-memoriam for my mother.'

Blizzard took the paper and saw that it was open at the deaths page. His attention was immediately drawn to an entry half-way down the third column and his eyes widened in astonishment.

'What does it say?' asked Colley.

'*Guthrie,*' read Blizzard. '*William James Died 30 August 1996.*'

'But he was only found three hours ago!' exclaimed Ross. 'There's no way they would have had time to get it in that quick, surely.'

'Unless whoever placed the ad knew what was going to happen.'

'Have you read the rest, sir?' asked the uniformed officer.

'*Gone and now he can be forgotten,*' said Blizzard. '*Rest in pieces, Billy.*'

'A misprint?' asked Ross, looking over the inspector's shoulder. 'It wouldn't be the first time.'

'Somehow,' said Blizzard, 'I think not.'

'Oh, before, I forget,' said the uniformed constable. 'The super's looking for you.'

'On a Saturday?' asked Blizzard, getting to his feet, 'Now why do I think that can only be something bad?'

Half an hour later, the storm having blown over, Blizzard and Detective Superintendent Arthur Ronald sat in the latter's office, the sunshine streaming in through the window and bathing the room in a golden light. For a few moments, neither man spoke amid the easy silence as they sipped at their mugs of tea. Ronald, a balding, slightly portly man dressed in a dark suit and with his tie done up even though it was a Saturday, had long been Blizzard's closest friend in the job. Their relationship went back to days spent working together as rookie detective constables, learning the trade on the housing estates of Hafton. After that, the men's careers had taken different paths. Blizzard remained in CID but Ronald went back into uniform, his easy manner and consummate people skills ensuring that he rose rapidly through the ranks.

The friends were reunited at Abbey Road when Ronald assumed command of CID in the constabulary's southern half and immediately demanded that Blizzard be moved from the drugs squad and promoted to detective chief inspector. It was a controversial suggestion because Blizzard's ability for ruffling feathers in the corridors of power had made him plenty of enemies at headquarters. However, the results had spoken for themselves: in the years that Blizzard had run Western CID, the previously spiralling crime rate had halted then dropped by twenty per cent and detection rates were up by a fifth. And the chief constable's beloved market research surveys had shown an increasing confidence in the police among local people. Some people said that it was this fact that kept John Blizzard in a job, immediately realizing the irony of the comment because everyone knew that the chief inspector hated the very idea of focus groups. 'If anyone wants to say something to me,' he would grumble whenever forced to attend such events, 'they've got my number. Nine, nine, sodding nine.'

It was a comment that went to the heart of the two men's very different characters. Blizzard, the college boy who went directly into the force and favoured direct speaking, Ronald, university educated, diplomatic and urbane, Blizzard with his tie always at half-mast, Ronald always smartly turned out, Blizzard the independent spirit who shied away from domestic responsibility, Ronald married with two teenaged children, a worrier of a man with eyes beneath which bags sagged darkly at the thought of university fees and his huge mortgage payments.

'So what brings you in on a Saturday?' asked Blizzard, taking a sip of tea. 'Your good lady wife threatening to take you shopping again?'

'I wish it was that easy,' sighed Ronald. 'Besides, she has made it abundantly clear that the only thing she wants to accompany her on her shopping trips is my credit card.'

'Surely it's not our murder then?'

'It has certainly intrigued me. I always wondered what happened to Billy Guthrie. I was in charge of Burniston when it all kicked off at the Queen's Head, you know. Nasty business. I heard that David brought someone in. A young girl, apparently?'

'Megan Rees.'

'The daughter?' said the superintendent, raising an eyebrow. 'Can't see that, John. Surely she's not the type.'

'You know her?'

'I saw at her father's funeral. She was only a kid when he died.'

'What about him? Did you know him?'

'I met him a couple of times at official dos for the Licenced Victuallers' Association. Pie and peas.'

'Ah, the glamour of high command.'

Ronald gave him a pained looked.

'Sorry,' said Blizzard. 'So what was he like?'

'Just a regular Joe. What happened to him was a real tragedy. But how come you've got his daughter in? Clutching at straws, isn't it?'

'Not when she was the one who found the body.'

The superintendent gave a low whistle.

'Difficult coincidence to explain,' he said.

'Yeah, but it still doesn't feel right,' said Blizzard, draining his mug and placing it on the desk. 'All too easy, Arthur.'

'Sometimes they are.'

'No. There's more to this one. I can feel it – and Ross says there is no forensic evidence which links her to the attack. Besides, how could a slight young woman like that be capable of smashing the living daylights out of a man like Billy Guthrie?'

'Maybe she had help.'

'Or maybe she didn't do it. Anyway, if our Mister Guthrie is not the reason for your appearance on a Saturday, might I ask what is? As if I didn't know.'

'The Spur.'

'Wondered if I might get the call, actually.'

'I think the chief felt that your diplomatic skills would be unsuited to keeping a lid on things,' said Ronald bleakly.

'Given your innate capacity to pick a fight when you're in a room on your own. Besides, you're hardly the estate's most popular human being.'

'I hear uniform are livid about what went off. The word is that they wanted to go in mob-handed.'

'The chief blocked it. I've just been at an emergency meeting at headquarters and it all got rather heated. Uniform are still adamant that they should be allowed to go in.'

'What did the chief say to that?'

'Have you ever seen a man disappear up his own jacksee?'

'I take it he's got cold feet then?'

'If he has, I imagine it's because they're sticking out of his arse.'

Blizzard roared with laughter: it was always the same on the very occasional moments when the superintendent resorted to vulgarities. Ronald gave him a rueful look.

'This is not a laughing matter,' he said but could not disguise his pleasure at the way the joke had been received.

'I take it that you reminded our beloved chief that we are here to nick villains?'

'Of course, but he went into his usual spiel. Risk of major disorder, blah blah, risk assessments blah blah, public safety considerations blah blah. I glazed over at that point.'

'Don't blame you,' said Blizzard, walking over to the kettle. 'Top up?'

'No thanks. Anyway, the upshot was that we cannot go in without good intelligence.'

'I'm sure if we asked the lads on the estate they would let us have the block of concrete back,' said Blizzard as he rooted round on the windowsill for the teabags. 'In fact, coming to think of it, isn't it embedded in one of our patrol cars?'

'Indeed.'

'Can you explain one thing to me?' said Blizzard, turning

with the box of teabags in the hand. 'The chief didn't object when we went into The Riverbeck last month. There must have been fifty officers that night. Colley reckons the joiner's still fixing the doors. So how come the chief's so twitchy about The Spur?'

'Kenny Jarvis.'

Blizzard stared at him.

'Really?'

'Yes, I was surprised as well. I didn't realize before today but the chief was hit really hard when Kenny died. As uniform were having a go at him this afternoon, he suddenly said he did not want another dead officer on his watch. Took the wind out of everyone's sails, I can tell you.'

Blizzard considered the comment, neither man speaking as both officers recalled the young constable stabbed and left to die in the stinking stairwell on The Spur. The chief inspector remembered the anger he had felt as he led the investigation into the murder and the savage satisfaction he experienced when he brought a gang of three youths off the estate to justice for the killing. But he also remembered, as always when he cast his mind back to those dark days, the sense of frustration that a lot of people on the estate knew a lot of things, decent people among them, but that none of them was prepared to talk to the police. The inspector recalled the way people could not wait to close their doors on his detectives as they conducted their inquiries. At the time, he had even tried to persuade Ronald that several people should be charged with obstructing the course of justice but his plea had fallen on deaf ears.

The inspector's mind strayed to the dead constable's distraught parents sitting in their living room as he tried to talk to them, the mother constantly twisting and untwisting her sodden handkerchief in her lap. And he recalled hardened officers sobbing uncontrollably at the funeral. As ever when he thought back on those days, he felt the strong emotions once again. Standing there, realizing that he still had the box of teabags in his hand, the inspector noticed Ronald eyeing him intently.

'I guess I can understand that,' said Blizzard with a grudging nod.

'Maybe you're not as different from the chief as you like to think.'

'I don't think so,' said Blizzard sharply. 'Just because we agree on this does not mean I agree with everything else the chief says.'

'God forbid,' murmured the superintendent.

'You and I have had this conversation a thousand times, Arthur,' said Blizzard, reaching out to check how warm the kettle was. 'We should not allow ourselves to be deflected from the right course of action just because some little toerag from The Spur—'

'Which is why you are here. You and I need to concoct a little plan.'

'Plan?'

'Yeah,' said the superintendent, lowering his voice even though they were alone in the office. 'One so good that not even the chief can stop us going on to that estate mob-handed.'

'Surely,' said Blizzard with a gleam in his eye, 'you are not conspiring against your own chief constable, Arthur? Man of your standing in the community, member of the Round Table and all that?'

'Just make it so good that not even the chief can refuse it.'

'Leave it to me,' beamed Blizzard.

A pensive Steve McGarrity stood on the front steps of the Railway Hotel, in Hafton city centre, and watched as Blizzard clambered out of the taxi. McGarrity sighed:

knowing his old friend as he did, he realized that it would not be long before the inspector started asking awkward questions, special occasion or not. McGarrity also knew that Blizzard would not let friendship stand in the way of his investigation into the death of Billy Guthrie. Seeing the determined way Fee Ellis and her male colleague had worked their way round the museum that afternoon, asking questions, taking statements, constantly on the lookout for anything out of the ordinary, had been enough to convince McGarrity of that.

Now, standing and watching his friend pay the driver, McGarrity heard laboured breathing behind him and turned to watch the approach across the foyer of Tommy Rafferty. McGarrity knew why he was breathing so hard: a life on the railways had taken its toll on many of the old railmen, the exposure to asbestos and coal dust relentlessly destroying the lining of their lungs. Rafferty's health had been steadily declining in recent years: it was, McGarrity had always thought, a high price to pay for a lifetime of devotion. A cruel mistress indeed, he had always felt. Always a strong union man, McGarrity had never failed to be angered by such thoughts.

However, tonight, other considerations occupied his mind as he watched Blizzard stop at the bottom of the steps to admire the large banner strung across the front of the Victorian hotel. THE RAILWAY HOTEL WELCOMES HAFTON RAILWAY APPRECIATION SOCIETY, it said. Even though its best days were far behind it, the hotel had been an appropriate choice for the organization's celebration dinner: built in 1847, it was only four years younger than Tenby Street railway station and the walls of its lounge were adorned with black-and-white photographs of old steam locomotives.

'Has he said anything?' asked Rafferty anxiously, coming to join his friend.

'Not yet, but he will. You know what he's like.'

'Perhaps he won't,' said Rafferty hopefully. 'He'll know we don't want to be dragged into something like this, not on a night like this. And we *are* his friends.'

'That is unlikely to make any difference,' said McGarrity, adding in a low voice. 'Perhaps we should give him something that he wants to hear instead. Take the heat off.'

Rafferty shot him an alarmed look.

'Trust me,' said McGarrity.

Taking another look at the banner, Blizzard smiled broadly: having freshened up at Abbey Road, he had headed directly to the hotel. Deep down, he knew that his place was with his investigators but the inspector had been looking forward to this night for months. For once, he was placing his personal life before duty. The realization made him feel uneasy but, in many ways, it felt like the culmination of a special phase of his life. His fascination with steam had started as a young boy but its roots stretched further back than that. Blizzard's grandfather had worked as a shedmaster in the locomotive sheds of industrial Yorkshire in the pre-war years, and his father worked for a while as a train driver. When his father's job took the family reluctantly north from rural Lincolnshire to grimy Hafton, the teenage Blizzard found that its status as one of the great railway cities compensated for the loss of village life. It was but a brief compensation because it was in Hafton in the sixties that a young John Blizzard witnessed the dying days of the golden age of steam.

He never forgot the sight of the retired locomotives left to rot in railway yards, and had long since resolved to do what he could to keep their memory alive. Having joined the city's police force, he had used his spare time to develop his passion for industrial history, particularly railways, a subject on which he was increasingly invited to address local groups in recognition of his expertise. There had even been suggestions that he write a book on the subject. Although the demands of the job gave him little opportunity to accept such opportunities, the fact that he had spent virtually all his career in Western Division did have its positives because his time conducting inquiries had given him the opportunity to explore the derelict sidings, trackways and tumbledown buildings that had once supported the city's railway industry but now stood on private land far from public view.

It was while investigating a serious assault that had taken place on wasteland a short distance from the Railway Hotel, that Blizzard had stumbled across the Silver Flyer, rusting away in an old shed. Hardly able to believe what he was seeing, he had contacted a number of local retired railmen and together they formed the Hafton Railway Appreciation Society, McGarrity the chairman, Blizzard the secretary and Rafferty the treasurer. After two years of fundraising, they bought the locomotive and embarked on the restoration, the work lovingly carried out in the shed. It had become a bolt-hole, somewhere to escape the pressures of life as a DCI. He had always marvelled at the way an hour's physical exertion on the locomotive had been able to clear his mind of dark thoughts. Ever since the job had been completed, the shed now standing empty, Blizzard had missed the experience.

Taking a final look at the banner, Blizzard surveyed the front of the hotel: he knew that once he got up to his room at the rear of the building, he would be able to look out over the wasteland and see the shed itself, empty, cold and silent now as it awaited the arrival of the society's next project. Its committee had already opened negotiations to purchase an old gasworks tank engine. The thought filled Blizzard with anticipation. The inspector noticed his friends at the top of the steps and bounded towards them, extending a welcoming hand.

'Gentlemen,' he said. 'Good to see you on an occasion such as this.'

Pleasantries exchanged, the three men walked into the hotel where the receptionist directed them down a gloomy corridor. On the way, Blizzard paused to look at one of the pictures, a series of locomotives lined up in a large workshop at the city's railway works. Standing next to them were rows of men with flat caps and clipped moustaches staring into the camera.

'A fine sight,' he said approvingly. 'The city lost so much when the works closed.'

'I keep telling you, it were a dirty, cold place to work,' grunted Rafferty.

'No romance,' said Blizzard, as they started walking down the corridor. 'Hey, Tommy, some fun and games at your place last night?'

'What do you mean?' Rafferty suddenly looked guarded.

'You know exactly what I mean. Someone tried to kill a couple of our officers on The Spur.'

'I keep out of it,' said Rafferty, wheezing hard and already lagging behind the other two. 'Don't make sense to get yourself involved. Don't want me windows smashing through.'

'God knows why you still live there, then.'

'I've lived there thirty years, John,' said Rafferty, stopping and stretching out a hand against the wall as he caught his breath. 'No low-life is going to drive me out.'

'Then help me.'

'It's bad enough that folks know that you and me are friends.'

Rafferty's body was suddenly racked by coughs and he bent double as he fought for breath.

'That enough romance for you?' murmured McGarrity.

Blizzard gave him a sharp look but said nothing.

'I'm all right,' said Rafferty, as the coughing eased. 'Come on.'

They resumed their walking.

'I really do need to know who dropped that concrete block on our car last night,' said Blizzard as they arrived at the door to the room in which the meal was to be served.

'Do you know how I have managed to live so many years in The Spur?' said Rafferty, making a zipping movement across his lips. 'I keep it shut.'

'In which case, what about the death of Billy Guthrie? Surely you—'

'And what's more,' said Rafferty, pushing his way into the room, 'you know better than to ask me.'

Blizzard sighed and looked at McGarrity, who shrugged. Over the next few minutes, the room filled up until there were more than forty men ready for their celebration meal, the air thick with the buzz of conversation and the wreathes of smoke curling from cigars kept for such a special occasion as this. Blizzard, sitting at the top table alongside McGarrity and Rafferty, surveyed the gathering affectionately. As the meal wore on, though, he was assailed by a dark thought. Surveying the weatherbeaten faces whose lines told a thousand tales, he could not push aside the idea that someone somewhere in their midst knew more than they were letting on about the death of Guthrie.

Blizzard dreaded the moment when he would have to destroy the happy atmosphere: did he have the right, he asked himself, to ruin an occasion which meant so much to all of them? Thought of his officers still working, of Colley missing another bath-time, Ramsey working his ninth late night in a row, brought the inspector to a sudden decision as the waitresses left having delivered the coffee. The inspector stood up and clinked on his wine glass with a fork to attract their attention. The murmur of conversation died away and the room fell silent.

'Gentlemen,' said Blizzard, 'this is indeed an occasion of which we should all be proud and Steve has asked me to say a few words, which my sergeant, a Philistine when it comes to such matters, would no doubt describe as "sentimental shite".'

A ripple of laughter ran round the room.

'And I promise not to use the word romance in case you resort to similar profanities about me.'

More laughter and there were a few claps. McGarrity grinned and reached up to pat the inspector affectionately on the shoulder.

'However,' said Blizzard, letting the laughter subside, his expression suddenly grave, 'before I call for the toast, I need, albeit reluctantly, to bring up a subject which I acknowledge should have no place at a celebration such as this.'

Uncomfortable looks spread round the room.

'I need help building up a picture of a man whose body was found near the museum this afternoon. Billy Guthrie.'

The name seemed to hang in the smoke-filled air but no one spoke. The seconds of silence lengthened.

'Come on, guys,' said Blizzard insistently, 'did anyone know him?'

Heads shook.

'Surely, some of you must have known him. He worked on the railways.'

'Don't mean he was one of us,' said one of the railmen.

'Come on, George, surely—'

'We don't want to get involved, John,' said the man, standing up and fixing the inspector with a stare.

Blizzard surveyed him for a moment: he did not really know George Haywood, who was dressed smartly in a suit with a carnation in the buttonhole, his thinning grey hair slicked back with gel. Blizzard seemed to recall that he had once worked in the city's locomotive works, and fancied that he might even have been a union shop steward, one of those who failed in the fight to save it from closure. Beyond that, Blizzard knew little. Haywood had joined the appreciation society more than a year after its formation but, although always courteous whenever they had met, had not offered to help with the refurbishment of the Old Lady. He had experienced enough of that in his working life, he had once said by way of explanation. That was enough for any man.

'Come on, George,' said Blizzard. 'Can you not—'

'I'll tell you this for nowt,' said Haywood, looking round the floor for support, 'you'll not be short of people glad to see the back of Billy Guthrie.'

One or two of the others nodded and some of the railmen stared uncomfortably into their pint glasses. Haywood sat down and took a defiant swig of his beer.

'Aye, best left dead,' said another voice but, hard as he looked, Blizzard could not see who had spoken.

'Come on, guys,' said Blizzard, his exasperation showing, 'I need more than this. This is a murder inquiry.'

The room fell silent again.

'I'll get there in the end.'

'Then you get there,' said another voice.

Blizzard nodded in defeat.

'OK,' he said held up his glass and gave a smile. 'Let's not allow Billy Guthrie to ruin this happy occasion. He wrecked enough things while he was alive, let's not give him the satisfaction of doing the same thing in death.'

The atmosphere in the room eased, men relaxed and there was a smattering of applause.

'We are here,' said Blizzard, glancing at the specially commissioned oil painting of the Silver Flyer which hung on the wall, 'to celebrate the unveiling of the Old Lady. Please, will you all be upstanding and raise your glasses in her honour.'

After the clinking of glasses and a round of applause, the rest of the evening went without incident amid anecdotes about the old days and much laughter and back-slapping until, one by one, the railmen weaved their way unsteadily out into the night. Shortly after midnight, Blizzard was perched on a stool at the deserted hotel bar, suddenly feeling weary and pondering whether or not to go up to his room: because he lived in a village to the west of the city and knew what kind of a night it would turn out to be, he had resolved some weeks previously to leave his car at Abbey Road. Not that the Railway Hotel was particularly pleasant – the rooms were spartan and smelled of damp – but at least it meant he would not have far to stagger. Peering moodily into the bottom of his glass, and wondering whether or not he should order another pint, he became aware of McGarrity approaching.

'We gave her a good send off then,' said Blizzard, smiling at his friend. 'Drink?'

'Aye, go on, lad.'

Blizzard ordered two more pints of bitter.

'I can't help thinking,' he said as he watched the barman pour the drinks, 'that we've lost something special tonight, Steve.'

'I thought you promised not to say romance,' said McGarrity, settling down on a stool. 'Besides, like you said, even if we don't get the gas loco there are plenty of others crying out for restoration. I do hear there's one in some farmer's field over Halethorpe way. Keeps his chickens in it, would you believe.'

'No, I don't mean that. I mean the people,' said Blizzard, nodding his thanks as the barman handed over their drinks.

'I looked round that room tonight, Steve, and I was the youngest by about twenty years. You know, sometimes in the summer myself and Fee go round the park on a Saturday afternoon and we stop and watch the blokes playing bowls. I look at those old guys and think "Jesus, when you're gone, what are we left with?"'

'Very profound,' said McGarrity taking a sip of his pint. 'I've never heard the drink more poetic.'

Blizzard gave a rueful smile. The men sat and drank in silence for a few moments then, when the barman went to clear some glasses from a table in the corner of the room, McGarrity leaned over towards his friend. Blizzard noticed that he seemed ill-at-ease.

'This did not come from me,' said McGarrity in a hesitant voice.

'All right.'

'I'm serious,' hissed McGarrity, glancing round as the barman returned. 'Let's sit at that table. I don't want to risk being overheard.'

Once they were seated, McGarrity looked at the inspector.

'You must promise that you will keep my name out of this,' he said earnestly.

Blizzard nodded.

'OK. Earlier on tonight, you asked about who might want to kill Guthrie,' said McGarrity. 'Well, maybe you should be looking at Lawrie Gaines.'

'And who?' asked Blizzard, taking a swig of his drink, 'is Lawrie Gaines?'

'You know that Billy Guthrie was a boxer?'

'Apparently.'

'Well, I used to follow the boxing a bit myself and I went to see him fight plenty of times. There was always a nasty side to Billy Guthrie. It made things more interesting.'

'What?' said the inspector with a slight smile as he took

another drink, 'You mean that boxers are normally being nice to each other when they try to stove their heads in?'

'There's a code, John, a code, but Guthrie never seemed to abide by it. He was a bit tapped, if you ask me. I was there the night he tried to make his comeback. He was up against Lawrie's brother, a local lad called Archie Gaines. He was just a kid.' McGarrity shook his head sadly at the memory. 'Just a kid.'

'I heard about this. Sounds like quite a night.'

'Aye, the place was packed. I'd never seen so many people crammed into the Victoria Hall. John, there must have been a thousand of them. And they were all there to see Guthrie. He had been a pretty decent fighter in his time and folks wanted to see if he still had it. I was pretty curious myself.'

'And had he?'

'Na,' and McGarrity shook his head. 'Before the fight most folks reckoned he would walk it easy but then he took his gown off and we realized that there was no way. He hadn't boxed for three years and there was no way he had done enough training. He had a beer belly, for God's sake. Typical Guthrie, mind. God, he was an arrogant bastard. Thought he could waltz in there and take the lad out.'

'I assume Archie was too good for him?'

'Too right he was. Must have been the best part of twenty-five years younger, fit as anything, quick as a jackrabbit. And he was a good technical fighter, was Archie. Knew how to punch. Billy Guthrie had no answer to him: you could see him getting more and more rattled as the fight wore on.'

'And?'

Billy Guthrie sat on his stool and stared at the baying mob crammed into the leisure centre's main hall. The atmosphere was rank with sweat and bad breath and the air was filled with the ugly sound of men yelling from twisted faces. Breathing hard from the exertions from the first four rounds, Guthrie felt light-headed and kept blinking to get rid of the blood trickling down from a gash above his right eye. He was aware of a dull ache in his abdomen where Gaines had landed a crushing blow in the first round, a punch that had sent the pain shooting through Guthrie's body, a blow that made him realize that he should not be there, that he could get himself badly hurt. Billy Guthrie was not used to being hurt.

'Come on, Billy,' hissed his trainer, sticking his face close to Guthrie's, 'he's fucking murdering you. You got to hit him back.'

'I can't do it,' whispered Guthrie. 'Throw the towel in, Roly.'

'No can do,' replied the trainer, and Guthrie noticed a strange look come into his eyes. 'Sorry, lad, you've got to see this one through.'

'What's happening,' asked the fighter sharply. 'What ain't you telling me, Roly?'

The trainer nodded to a short man sitting in the front row of the audience, watching their conversation intently. Black hair thinning even though he was only in his early thirties, the man was dressed in a sharp black suit, as were the large men sitting either side of him.

'What's it got to do with him?' asked Guthrie, alarm in his voice.

The trainer hesitated.

'Tell me!' snarled Guthrie.

'He's got money on you to win,' murmured Roly, glancing round furtively lest anyone else hear. 'Big money.'

Guthrie closed his eyes and felt a sudden vicious throbbing in his head. He opened his eyes again and surveyed the baying crowd.

'Why didn't you tell me?' he croaked.

'I didn't think it mattered. I reckoned the kid would give you the runaround for a couple of rounds then you'd deck him.' He looked at Guthrie accusingly. 'You assured me you'd put the roadwork in.'

'How much?' asked Guthrie, noticing the referee walking over towards them and hissing with extra urgency in his voice. 'How much has he got on me, Roly?'

'Plenty.'

'Come on, lads, are you going to fight?' asked the referee, peering at Guthrie's battered features and half-closed right eye. 'Or do you want to hand it to the kid?'

Guthrie glanced back to the man in the audience and his shaven-headed heavies. The man fixed him with a stare.

'Well?' asked the referee. 'You done?'

'No,' sighed Guthrie, struggling to his feet, 'I'm OK.'

'You sure?' asked the referee. 'He's running rings round you, Billy.'

'I'm OK,' snarled Guthrie.

'Well, I'm warning you, if he hits you with another couple of punches like he did at the end of last round, I'll have to stop it.'

'I said I was all right.'

The referee shrugged. Breathing hard, feeling as if everything was happening far away, Guthrie took a few steps into the ring. Archie Gaines, tall and lean, danced towards him, and Guthrie did not even see the first punch as it tore through his defences and slammed into his face. Vision stained red with blood, Guthrie grunted and sunk to his knees. The sound of the mob seemed to come from another world and he felt his stomach heave. In that moment, he realized how his many victims had felt, sensed the day he had always known would come, the day when someone got the better of him. But in that moment, he knew that whatever it took, this was not that day. Not at the hands of some spotty kid.

Guthrie hauled himself to his feet. With an enraged bellow, he lunged forward and smashed his head into the startled boy's face. Gaines swayed for a moment, his eyes registering his shock. Guthrie snapped out a fist and delivered a powerful uppercut followed by a thunderous haymaker. There was a gasp as the crowd heard the cracking of bones and Gaines swayed again for a moment, his features frozen in shock, his eyes wide, his mouth hanging open, the blood pouring from his shattered nose and his arms dangling loose at his side. As the referee stepped quickly forward, Guthrie brushed aside his restraining arm, gave a snarl and advanced on his opponent once more to unleash a final blow. Gaines staggered backwards, blood spattered the air, then his knees gave way and with a sigh he collapsed to lie still on the canvas, lifeless eyes staring up at the ceiling. Guthrie leapt into the top rope and punched the air in exultation.

'Fucking come on!' he bellowed, ignoring the horrified expressions in the front row. 'Fucking come on!'

'I have never seen anything like it,' said McGarrity with a shake of the head. 'The man was an animal.'

He took a deep drink of beer as if it would somehow banish the memories of that night, watched in silence by Blizzard.

'I tell you, John, I thought the kid was dead,' said McGarrity. 'Everyone thought he was dead.'

'What happened after that?'

'The place erupted. There was folks trying to bring the poor kid round and some people trying to climb into the ring to get at Guthrie. Typical of the man, mind, because he squared up to them, landed a couple of punches. I'll give him something, he had courage.'

'I don't think that's the right word for bullies like him. What happened next?'

'Guthrie got himself out through a back door in the end. 'Course it was the end for him – he was given a lifetime ban. Mind, he had disappeared by then, so not sure it made much difference.'

'And you reckon there was a lot of money on the fight?'

'I'm just telling you what I heard,' said McGarrity, adding quickly, 'Nothing was ever proved, mind.'

'But you knew?'

'Everyone knew, John.'

'And this guy on the front row, what was his name?'

McGarrity did not reply and Blizzard thought he detected a hint of fear in his eyes.

'Come on, Steve,' said the inspector. 'You know I'll keep it in confidence.'

'You make sure you do,' hissed McGarrity, glancing around even though the bar was empty and the barman had left the room carrying some glasses, 'because if you don't, you'll end up fishing me out of the canal. It was Eddie Gayle.'

'Now there,' said Blizzard, his eyes gleaming, 'is a thing.'

'Just keep me out it.'

'I will. It's a while since Eddie Gayle and I have had a nice cosy chat. And Archie Gaines? What happened to him after the fight?'

'Kid tried to go back to work. He was a lathe worker. Only lasted a few days. My mate worked with him, said that they had to lay him off. The lad was a liability. A couple of weeks later, he had some sort of stroke or something and that was that.'

'And the brother – what did Lawrie do?'

'The word was that there was a set-to with Guthrie in the changing room after the fight. Folks reckon Lawrie threatened to kill Guthrie but it could have been pub talk. Mind, Lawrie always was a hothead. Maybe he finally carried through with it. Maybe that's why you found Guthrie today.'

'Possible, I suppose,' said Blizzard, taking another swig of his pint. 'But if he was going to have done it, he would have done it a long time ago, surely.'

'Yeah, but Guthrie vanished, remember. Besides, there's something else you should know. See, Archie's dad took it all really hard, died a couple months later. Folks said it was of a broken heart. You know how people say these things. Anyway, after the dad dies, Lawrie reckoned he could not look after his brother. Felt really guilty about it but the kid had to go into a home. Not around here, over in the Midlands somewhere.' McGarrity paused for effect. 'I heard that he died three weeks ago. And that means Lawrie Gaines has lost both of them because of what happened that night.'

With that, he downed his pint and walked unsteadily from the room. Blizzard stared after him then glanced at his watch, fished his mobile phone out of his jacket pocket and dialled a number.

'Sorry to ring at this hour,' he said.

'No bother,' said Colley, glancing down at the baby lying on the floor, watching his every movement with beady eyes. 'We are watching Cagney and Lacey. Say hello to your godfather, Laura.'

'Hello, Laura,' said Blizzard down the phone, grinning foolishly. 'Listen, when you were doing the background checks into Guthrie tonight, did the name Lawrie Gaines crop up?'

'You talking to me or the baby?'

The sergeant heard the inspector's low laugh down the phone.

'You,' said Blizzard. 'So did Lawrie Gaines's name come up?'

'Yeah,' said the sergeant. 'Ross mentioned him. Brother of the kid who got hurt in that boxing match. What of it?'

'Turns out that Archie Gaines died three weeks ago and I'm wondering if that makes the brother our main suspect for Billy Guthrie.'

'We'll add him to the list.'

'List? Are there others?'

'You have no idea,' said Colley. 'Three of us spent tonight tracking down some of the people who had fallen foul of Guthrie. I tell you, guv, this guy made enemies like the rest of us have pints of beer, which from the sound of your voice you have done tonight.'

'I'm not drunk,' said Blizzard but was acutely conscious that his voice had slurred as he said it.

'Course not.'

'Anyway,' said the inspector, 'drunk or sober, I reckon Lawrie Gaines has got to be worth a tug.'

'Ahead of you on that one. We checked the house but it was deserted. I've got people keeping an eye on it.'

'Are we any nearer to tracing Guthrie's movements?'

'We have had one or two reports suggesting that he might have come back to the city on Thursday night, the day before the murder. But quite what he was doing, we're not sure at the moment.'

'So where was he between then and when he got killed?'

'Not sure of that either. The reports are from different parts of the city.'

'I'm going to go back to the factory and see what's happening,' said Blizzard, downing his pint and slamming it on the table so loudly that the barman glanced over at him.

'No need, guv. It's all in hand and they're going to ring me if Lawrie Gaines turns up. I reckon the other things can wait 'til morning. Besides, Cagney has just arrested the villain so there's no need to worry.'

Blizzard looked down at his empty glass.

'Maybe you're right,' he said and a thought struck him. 'What time did you get home?'

'About an hour ago.'

'You'll be popular.'

'Could say that,' said the sergeant, glancing across at the baby. 'Anyway, got to go, there's a strange whiff in the air and I'm pretty sure it's not me.'

Blizzard shuddered and walked over to order another drink from the barman.

chapter seven

U nable to sleep, John Blizzard stood at the window of his hotel room and stared down into the street. Acutely aware that he had consumed far too much ale than was good for a man of his age, he had resolved to go straight to bed. However, because the Railway Hotel stood in the heart of the city centre, the inspector had struggled to sleep amid the shouts and banging doors as the clubs spewed their drunken clientele into the night. After lying and listening to the Saturday night hubbub for half an hour, the inspector had given a frustrated grunt and padded over to the sink where he had poured a glass of water in a desperate attempt to head off the hangover he knew would surely follow his excesses. Then he walked over to the window to watch the revellers making their way home along streets slicked with rain.

Blizzard allowed himself a slight smile as he saw two young men in white T-shirts falling to blows, embarking on the pantomime that only drunken men can enact when fighting, staggering and swaying as they aimed punches that would never find their target and shouting obscenities garbled by beer. Watching the scuffle, Blizzard recalled his conversation with Steve McGarrity in the bar an hour previously and was struck by the stark contrast with the boxing match that had ruined Archie Gaines's life. As long as these drunks fought, they would not injure each other, probably would not even remember it, Blizzard knew that, but what had happened in Victoria Hall had been different. Savage. Animal. The inspector had never understood sport – had never tried – but he realized that the fight had crossed the boundaries governing those taking part. What was it McGarrity had called it? The code? Clearly, Guthrie had not respected the code but could his death twelve years later really be a simple case of revenge from a brother who had bided his time? Was Ronald right, Blizzard wondered as he peered out of the window? Was murder sometimes as simple as it comes? And it was easy enough to concoct the scenario: Guthrie comes back to the city, Lawrie Gaines sees him entirely by chance in the street, lures him to the signal box then ... No, and Blizzard shook his head. No, it just did not sound right.

And what of Megan Rees, the inspector asked himself as he took a sip of water then watched in amusement as one of the drunks staggered backwards to stumble over the kerb and sprawl in the road? Where did she fit into things? They could not both have killed Guthrie, surely? Or could they? Vengeful children taking revenge on the killer of their loved ones? Nice angle yet none of the detectives had turned up anything to link Megan Rees with any of the Gaines family. And what of Eddie Gayle, what was his role in the story? Sure, he was capable of murder, Blizzard knew that. Or rather he was capable of ordering murder: the city's underworld had always been rife with the rumours and half-truths about the terrible exploits of Eddie Gayle and his gangland associates. But over a bet in a boxing match? Much as Blizzard wanted to believe it, he doubted it was the answer.

Seeing a taxi swerve to avoid the young man in the road, the inspector peered to his right and saw three uniformed officers walking briskly across from where they had been watching the fight. The possibility that the man might get himself killed under the wheels of a car had sparked them into action and, watching them drag him to his feet and begin to calm down his opponent, while talking to the other young men who had now started to gather round the confrontation, Blizzard was reminded of his days as a young uniformed officer. Blizzard had hated every minute of uniformed life, and had done everything in his power to escape it, but there was nevertheless something about witnessing the uniforms at work that brought about a sense of nostalgia. Standing in the hotel room, his face illuminated by the flashing blue lights of the van that had appeared down below, he found himself recalling those days with something approaching affection.

'Too much bloody drink,' muttered the inspector.

And went back to bed.

It was just after two when McGarrity's phone rang. Fumbling in the darkness for the bedside light switch, he glanced at the clock and groaned.

'Who is this?' he asked, picking up the phone.

'You know who it is,' replied a voice. 'Tell me that you succeeded?'

'I did my best, George. Told him to go after Lawrie Gaines.'

'Let's hope he does, then,' said the voice. 'The last thing we want is the bastard sniffing around us.'

The line went dead. McGarrity's wife rolled over and peered blearily at her husband.

'Who was that?' she asked.

'Wrong number. Thought we were a taxi company. Go back to sleep, Margaret.'

But it was only when the first rays of dawn were streaking the sky that Steve McGarrity finally slipped into a fitful slumber and even then it was one haunted by the ghosts of the past.

As the rain squalled in off the River Haft and drifted across the sleeping city, two men in dark clothing walked slowly and carefully across the wasteland, making sure that their feet made little sound on the shards of broken bottles as they headed towards the railway siding. Clambering up the embankment, they dropped down on to the trackbed and walked along the siding in the direction of the railway museum, their progress illuminated by the dim glow from the street lights on nearby terraced streets.

Finding themselves at the perimeter fence of the museum, the men crouched down and there was a snipping sound as one of them cut a hole in the wire. Crawling through, they advanced quickly on the building and disappeared into the shadows around the back, still moving carefully lest they trigger any security lights. None came on. One of the men glanced down at his luminous watch: 0.45 a.m., it said. They clambered on to a shed attached to the main building then hoisted themselves up to the roof, clinging precariously on to the drainpipe running up the side of the building. Once or twice it creaked and they froze, suspended in mid-air, hardly daring to breathe lest it give way and hurl them to the ground. Satisfied that it would hold their weight, they continued to climb and within a few short moments were at the top.

Edging their way carefully across the sloping tiled roof, they eventually reached the highest point and took a moment or two to survey the scene around them: in one direction they looked out over rows of terraced streets stretching into the distance, the houses interspersed by the dull shapes of factories and office blocks. Looking the other way, the men could see how close they were to the city centre, could see the street lights and hear the hum of traffic, the slamming of car doors and the occasional shout as the clubs turned out and the taxis starting ferrying the drunken revellers home after a Saturday night on the lash. Looking down, the men saw, briefly glimpsed through the trees, a man walking unsteadily along the street on the far side of the wasteland. For a few moments, he turned and looked directly towards the museum but the wooded belt shielded the intruders from view and after a few seconds he continued his slightly unsteady journey.

Returning their attention to the job in hand, the men edged over to one of the skylights, taking great care because the roof was increasingly slippery with the falling rain. They peered down into the shadows of the railway museum for a few moments, just able to make out in the glow afforded by a series of low lights around the walls the dull forms which they knew to be railway engines and display cases.

'That's the Silver Flyer,' said one of the men, pointing to the engine, which had been reversed into its resting place at the end of the museum closest to the large double doors. 'Can we get in without triggering the alarm?'

'Piece of cake,' nodded his accomplice, peering through the skylight. 'Them doors at the end don't look very secure. All we have to do is get them open and back the truck in. Mind, it don't look that special. Is our man right?'

'He reckons some of that pipework is worth a packet. Besides, think how pissed off it will make Blizzard.'

'Well, it looks easy enough,' said the accomplice. 'When are we going to come back and—?'

Before he could complete the sentence, he lost his footing and, with a horrified look on his face, slid silently, wordlessly, down to the edge of the roof, feet scrabbling on the tiles, hands grasping desperately for a hold before he disappeared into the void. His friend heard a dull thud as he struck the ground. Then all was silence.

Six-thirty in the morning found John Blizzard sitting in a taxi bound for work. The inspector had spent a disturbed night at the hotel. When he did finally get to sleep, it was to dream of Billy Guthrie's battered features, steam locomotives that never seemed to reach their destination and Megan Rees with that knowing smile on her face. Waking shortly after six, and nursing a severe headache that seemed to get worse with every movement, Blizzard had scrabbled around for the Anadin in his jacket pocket and showered. Trying to ignore the pain, he had gingerly walked downstairs, settled his bill – ignoring the knowing smile of the young girl on reception – and headed for the taxi rank outside the station where he asked the only cab driver there to take him to Abbey Road.

Blizzard had spent most of his career at Abbey Road. Constructed as a temporary measure in the 1960s, the single-storey station was still there three decades later, its corridors snaking in a rough octagonal shape, the green paint on its prefabs peeling and the roof leaking. Its main advantage, though, was its location, well placed for the officers tasked with policing Western Division. Situated amid a pleasant middle-class residential area, Abbey Road lay at the heart of the division: to its south the River Haft, to its east the city centre, to its north the expanse of Victorian terraced houses that were virtually all now bedsits, and fanning out to the west, mile upon mile of run-down sixties council estates with shuttered corner shops, burnt-out cars and abandoned pushchairs. Sitting in the back seat of the taxi, Blizzard gazed silently out of the window at the passing houses and tried to think about something else than his throbbing skull.

'You have a few last night?' asked the driver.

'Why do you ask?'

'Because you look like shit.'

'Not been on a customer relations course then?' said Blizzard.

The cab arrived at the station well before seven and, feeling like death, the inspector sat in his office trying to study the reports from the night before while waiting for the Anadin to take effect. Occasionally, he winced as a particularly vicious stabbing sensation bored its way into his brain. Sipping at a glass of water, he constantly reminded himself, as he always did whenever this happened, that he was too old for all-night drinking. With the pain refusing to ease, and unable to read the reports in the half-light offered by his desk lamp (the inspector felt that the main light would be too painful an experience for a man in his condition), Blizzard cursed and threw the document down on to the desk. Glancing over to another pile of reports, he noticed that the top one dealt with the incident on The Spur two nights previously.

He found his mind drifting back, as it did so often, to that dark night on the estate. The inspector had been working late and was about to leave for home when the call came in. The news that a constable had been murdered had electrified the police station and, as Blizzard strode out on his way to the car park, Abbey Road's corridors were full of shocked officers and civilians, desperate to do something but able to do nothing. Sitting now in his dimly lit office, the inspector could smell again the acrid stench of the urine as he walked into the stairwell on The Spur, past a knot of grim-faced officers, and made his way up through the darkness to the first floor. Kenny Jarvis was sprawled several steps below the landing, face white, eyes staring, blood welling from the stab wound to his chest.

Blizzard had stood and stared down at him for a few moments, almost unable to take the scene in. Despite two decades in the job, he had never seen the body of a murdered police officer before. Bodies, yes, of course, but they had not meant much to him, just another lost identity, another case, a name on a file. But this had been different, he had known Kenny Jarvis, had exchanged pleasantries with him whenever they passed each other in the corridor at Abbey Road, had answered his hopeful questions about a possible move to CID. Staring down at the body, Blizzard had felt not just an overwhelming grief – young, oh so young – but also a huge sense of responsibility. He recalled glancing along the landing at the uniforms holding back a gaggle of rubberneckers, then walking over to the balustrade and looking down on the upturned faces of the officers gathered in the quadrangle. Blizzard remembered how he was assailed by the overpowering realization that each and every one of them was looking for him to solve the crime and solve it fast. Without realizing it as he sat in his office now, the inspector clenched his fist at the memory.

Hearing the sounds of the station coming to life, he sighed, stood up, wincing again at the pain from his head, and walked slowly down to the CID room where officers were starting to come in. Dragging up a chair at the front, he let his gaze roam round the room. Standing at the filing cabinet in the corner, flicking through papers, was Ramsey. Close by sat Colley, tipping back on a chair, eyes closed as he tried to catch up with some sleep: Laura had not fallen into slumber on his lap until 3.30 and the sergeant had woken to an Open University physics programme he did not understand.

In front of the sergeant sat Fee Ellis and she caught the inspector's eye, laughing out loud when he tried to wink then winced as another shaft of pain jagged its way round his head. 'Piss-pot,' she mouthed. The inspector nodded ruefully and glanced round the rest of the room at several other young detective constables and, sitting by the window, Dave Tulley, a tubby black-haired sergeant in his twenties, dressed as ever in a poorly fitting dark suit with crumb flecks down the jacket as he munched on a pastie.

'You OK, guv?' asked Ramsey.

'Just tell me where we are,' grunted the inspector.

He allowed himself a slight smile as the younger officers tried to look busy, flicking through their pocket books or rustling papers: Blizzard loved having a reputation.

'Where we are,' said Colley, still not opening his eyes, 'is that they were queuing up to stick one on Billy Guthrie.'

'And who's at the head of the queue? Lawrie Gaines?'

'He's certainly worth looking at, not least because he has gone AWOL,' said Ramsey, turning away from the filing cabinet. 'No one has been at the house all night. And Lawrie Gaines has not been seen for a couple of days, apparently. Maybe you can help with that, guv. I understand you gathered some intelligence on him last night during what we might describe as covert inquiries?'

Blizzard looked at him for a moment, wondering if the detective inspector was joking: Ramsey attempting humour always threw him off guard. However, the DI retained a deadpan expression and Blizzard gave up trying to work it out.

'Something like that,' he said.

The other officers checked to see he was taking the comment in the right spirit then allowed themselves to laugh; you always had to be careful with John Blizzard, they all knew that. And he did have a hangover, which was guaranteed to blacken his mood. Only Colley laughed without checking.

'Lawrie certainly has motive,' said Ramsey, reaching on to

a desk for a brown file. 'After his brother got injured in the fight, East CID were called in to investigate but, for some reason, it was decided to leave the matter in the hands of the boxing authorities. Not sure that was a particularly wise decision. OK, so Guthrie got a life ban but I would argue that what he did was assault and should have been dealt with by the court.'

'I would agree,' nodded Blizzard. 'Mind you, knowing Guthrie as we do, there's a good chance that a thousand people would have claimed to be looking the other way when it happened.'

Ramsey nodded gloomily.

'Have we found out if it's true that the kid died three weeks ago?' asked Blizzard.

'I've been ringing around,' said Tulley, consuming the last of his pastie and shying the paper bag at the nearby bin. 'But without knowing which home he went to, it's taking longer than I expected. None of Lawrie's neighbours know.'

'The real problem,' said Colley, finally opening his eyes, 'is that Lawrie Gaines is not the only one with good reason to want to see Billy Guthrie dead.'

'Yeah,' nodded Ramsey, reaching for another pile of papers on the desk. 'I had Burniston send down their stuff – there's at least three people sustained serious injuries at his hands during pub brawls in the 1980s all without anything ever coming to court. We talked to two of them last night and are waiting on a call about the third one. Oh, and you can add the family of Denny Rees to that as well, of course. There's plenty of people still hacked off that Guthrie never faced court over that one.'

'Perhaps that's as much our fault as theirs,' said the inspector.

The officers looked at him uneasily. Blizzard was renowned for his honesty, even if his views did upset the top brass, and among the comments which had concerned senior officers most were his outspoken pronouncements on the subject of witnesses who declined to go to court. It was, the inspector had always argued, their civic duty to come forward and give statements, fear of intimidation or not. He had made his views known at a public forum a couple of years previously, attracting negative headlines in the local paper, prompting a lively debate in the letters column and earning himself a rebuke from the chief constable. Not that the warning deferred him from pronouncing on the subject from time to time, which unsettled officers when he started to voice his views. All except Chris Ramsey, whose job included liaising with the local branch of Victim Support.

'Surely,' said Ramsey: the two men had disagreed many times on the subject, 'you cannot really be suggesting that Guthrie was allowed to do these things because folks let him? The man was a psycho.'

'Psycho or not, he got away with it for too long,' and Blizzard tried to strike a more conciliatory tone, eager to avoid an argument for the sake of both the murder inquiry and his aching head. Mainly his aching head: he was already regretting saying anything. 'And we don't come out of this smelling of roses, do we? The man was a thug and we should have made sure he was locked up.'

Ramsey said nothing: he did not want a row either, not with so much work to do.

'And on the theme of thugs,' said Blizzard, 'let me throw in another name with connections to Guthrie.'

They looked at him expectantly. Blizzard let the silence lengthen: he loved making an impact.

'Eddie Gayle,' he said eventually. 'Another one who should have been locked up a long time ago.'

There was silence as the officers digested the information.

Everyone knew that the chief inspector and Eddie Gayle went way back.

'And where exactly does he fit into it?' asked Ramsey doubtfully, glancing down at the documents piled up on the desk. 'His name has not cropped up in any of our inquiries so far.'

'He had money on the fight in which Archie Gaines was injured. When Guthrie lost his rag and headbutted the kid, it cost Eddie Gayle a pretty packet.'

'Sorry, guv, but it's weak,' said Ramsey.

'Maybe it is, but it's still worth considering.'

'Depends where it comes from.'

'Covert inquiries,' said Blizzard with a slight smile.

There was a low murmur of laughter and the atmosphere relaxed. Ramsey nodded ruefully.

'Do you want me to bring him in?' he asked.

'What, and ruin my fun?'

There was a ripple of laughter round the room, louder this time.

'Besides, bringing him in now would be a mistake,' said the inspector, 'We need more. More on everything really. Fee, anything from the people at the museum yesterday?'

'Not really. We came across a couple of guys who knew Guthrie, but same old story, I am afraid – the moment we asked them to elaborate, their memories failed them.'

'What is clear, though,' said Colley, 'is that Guthrie was a busy little bee after he came back to the city, probably on Thursday. We've got reports from several people in our area now. A couple saw him in the street and he was seen buying something from a corner shop. Oh, and East have been on – they reckon they have got a report over on their side as well.'

'So what was he doing?' mused Blizzard. 'What would bring him back after all these years?'

'Knowing Guthrie, he came back to settle some old scores,' said Ramsey.

'But why now?'

Ramsey shrugged.

'What about the death notice in the newspaper?' asked the inspector, looking round the room. 'Do we know who put that in the paper yet?'

'I got someone from the advertising department,' said Tulley. 'Bit dim, if you ask me. When I pointed out that the phraseology was a bit disrespectful, she said she hadn't noticed.'

'And do you believe her?'

'Well, she was a blonde,' said Tulley, then noticing Fee's sharp expression, clapped a hand to his mouth and stared in horror at the chief inspector. 'Not that I'm saying that blonde girls are, I mean, what I meant to say is that she ... they ...'

The sergeant's voice tailed off.

'Without digging yourself any deeper,' said Blizzard, 'what about the person who placed the ad?'

'Ah, yes, well,' said Tulley, flicking furiously through his notes. 'This, er, this very intelligent young girl reckoned that the ad was placed by a relative. A young girl. However, when we checked the details, the name and address are fake and the credit card was set up using the same bogus ID. The forensic boys are trying to find anything that links it to Megan Rees.'

'But,' said Graham Ross, walking into the room, 'we haven't. We went back to her house, like you said, guv, but there's nothing there.'

'However, she does have good reason to kill him,' and Blizzard stood up, his headache starting to ease. 'Fee, let's go and see what a night's sleep has done for her. I hope it was better than mine.'

Ten minutes later, they were sitting in the interview room, looking across the table at Megan Rees, who returned their gaze with her customary calm expression. However, there was a difference from the last time they had seen her: the bags under her eyes suggested that she had slept little in the cramped cell and gave the officers their first sense that she was under more strain than she was showing outwardly.

'A somewhat obvious trick,' said Megan, gesturing at Fee Ellis. 'What's the thinking, Blizzard? That I'll somehow crack and pour my heart out to a woman? Did you really think that would work?'

Blizzard sighed: this was not going to be easy.

'The doctor,' he said, glancing down at a piece of paper on the desk, 'seems to think that you should be sectioned. At least until we can find out if there has been a recurrence of your illness.'

'Well, there hasn't.'

'The report says,' continued Blizzard, ignoring the comment, 'that you exhibit pronounced mood swings and a pathological disregard for the death of Billy Guthrie.'

'I'm not sure pathological is the right word. I can tell the difference between right and wrong. It's just that I happen to think that what happened to Billy Guthrie was justified.'

'According to your records, it would not be the first time that a psychiatrist has expressed such concerns about your state of health. There's a report here from a chap called Johnston—'

'Him.' snorted Megan. 'He wanted his way with me, that's what that was about. The man was an old lech.'

'Be that as it may, I cannot ignore the fact that you exhibit—'

'Come on, Blizzard. I am sure that your inquiries have revealed plenty of other people who would agree with me about Guthrie. Some of your officers among them, I suspect. Does that make them mad as well?'

'I have to go with what the doctor says.'

'An easy line to come out with,' she said, eyeing him keenly, 'but what do you think, Chief Inspector? Do you think I am some kind of deranged madwoman?'

'I think that you are as sane as they come, Miss Rees.'

'Then why not let me go?'

'I am afraid I cannot do that.'

'Why?' Her voice had an edge to it.

'Because your sanity makes you all the more interesting to me. I think you are a calculating woman who is perfectly capable of murder – and you have just told me that you think Guthrie's death was justified. Until I can work out your little game, you are going nowhere.'

'What?' protested Megan, her sense of control disturbed. 'You haven't got enough to hold me so you're going to bang me up in a nuthouse until you have? How crap is that? And probably illegal.'

Blizzard did not reply.

'And you?' said Megan, looking suddenly at Ellis. 'What do you think? Do you think I am a disgrace to the fairer sex, Fee?'

'I think you need to remember where you are,' said the constable sharply. 'This is a murder inquiry.'

Megan said nothing.

'Besides,' said Blizzard wearily, tiring of the verbal jousting and standing up, the chair legs scraping on the floor. 'It's not my decision any more. It's down to the shrink. Of course, I could put a word in for you if you co-operate with our inq—'

'Another somewhat cheap shot, Chief Inspector. Me a vulnerable young lady and you an experienced detective trying to bully a confession out of me?' The voice was mocking. 'What would a good lawyer make of that?'

'Pity you declined our offer of one.'

'I didn't know you were the kind of police officer to play games with innocent young women. I thought you were better than that.'

Blizzard closed his eyes but, for the first time in two hours, he realized that his headache had disappeared. So intense had been the conversation he had not noticed the pain vanish. Suddenly feeling more human, he opened his eyes again, sat down and fixed Megan with an icy stare. Taken aback, she sensed that something had changed and, for the first time, uncertainty showed in her eyes. Fee glanced over at the inspector: the old John Blizzard was back.

'Time to cut the games, Megan,' said the inspector, a new edge to his voice. 'I want answers and I want them now before some quack stuffs you into a loony bin and throws away the key. Did you kill Billy Guthrie?'

Megan shook her head quickly.

'No,' she said, 'no, I did not.'

'Does the name Lawrie Gaines mean anything to you?'

Again the question was snapped out and again she shook her head.

'And what about Archie Gaines? Have you ever heard of—?'

The question was interrupted by a knock on the door and Blizzard looked up irritably as Colley walked in.

'What?' snapped the inspector.

'Sorry, guv,' said the sergeant, 'but before you continue the interview, there's something you really do need to see.'

Megan Rees gave them both a worried look.

'I think,' she said, 'that I would like that lawyer now.'

chapter eight

Blizzard got out of the car and he and Colley stood looking out across the wasteland near the railway siding. The inspector scowled: it was always the same when he came here and saw the scene of desolation. Ever since the houses had been bulldozed, the area had become a haunt for fly-tippers. The inspector looked at the sofa standing in the middle of the wasteland. Difficult to tell what colour it had been, he thought gloomily, red perhaps. Close by, he noticed a couple of equally grubby armchairs and someone with a sense of humour had placed an old standard lamp next to them. It created a surreal picture, almost as if the living room was still there and the house had been bulldozed around the occupants, thought Blizzard. The inspector let his gaze roam further across the wasteland. Colley followed the inspector's gaze and sighed as he noticed a burned-out car and Blizzard's eyes narrowed. *One*, thought the sergeant, *two*, I'll give it to three....

'What's that bloody thing doing there?' said the inspector.
Three.

'I thought the council was supposed to get rid of torched cars,' continued the inspector irritably. 'I seem to recall seeing half a million sodding memos about it from some stuffed shirt at headquarters. Multi-Agency Arson Task Force and all that malarkey. I even had to go to some damn-fool meeting about it. I mean, what's the point if nobody does anything about it? If you ask me, we should—'

'Indeed we should,' interrupted Colley, stepping out on to the wasteland, his shoes crunching on broken glass. 'It's over here.'

'I mean, look at it,' continued the inspector, vaguely waving a hand as he followed the sergeant. 'The railway company built these houses for its workers. And over there was the locomotive works. And just beside it was the first railway shed to be constructed in Hafton. It's a car wash now.'

The inspector caught his colleague up.

'We're losing it, David, he said earnestly. 'We're losing it.'

'I certainly am,' muttered the sergeant.

Blizzard was about to reply but something in the detective's demeanour counselled silence. The inspector had learnt that silence was the best way to deal with the flashes of irritation that had become more and more frequent since the birth of the sergeant's baby. So, without speaking, the detectives approached three uniformed officers standing around a crouching Graham Ross in the middle of the wasteland. The forensics chief turned to face them and held up, in a gloved hand, the muddy remains of a credit card that had appeared to have been the subject of a crude attempt to slice it through. Blizzard peered at it.

'This definitely the one?' he asked dubiously.

'It's the one used to book the newspaper advert,' nodded Ross. 'Someone tried to obscure the details but it's the same fake name. And Dave says that Megan Rees walks her dog over this area every day. Got to put her in the frame.'

'Half the dog owners in Hafton walk their dogs across here,' protested Blizzard.

'Yes, I know, but surely the fact that the credit card has—'

'I don't buy it,' said Blizzard with a shake of the head as he peered closer at the card. 'I mean, ask yourselves for a start – how come we didn't find it the first time we searched the area yesterday afternoon?'

'Sometimes people miss things,' said Ross.

'I reckon someone put it there for us to find. A somewhat crude attempt at that. I mean, it's all too easy.'

'Sometimes murders are,' pointed out Ross.

'You sound like Ronald,' grunted the inspector.

'Maybe he's got a point,' said Colley. 'Our last four have been sorted within twenty-four hours, remember. In fact, it was you who complained the other day that we weren't having to do any thinking. I seem to recall you giving your lecture on the lack of ingenuity in the modern murderer. Said you were going to write an academic paper on it when you retired. Whatever happened to good old-fashioned murders? you said.'

'Not this one,' said Blizzard firmly. 'I think we're missing something.'

'Missing what?'

'If I knew that, it wouldn't be missing.'

A shout attracted their attention and they saw a man running from the direction of the museum.

'Who is he?' asked Colley, glancing at the inspector.

'Malcolm Watt. The museum manager.'

'He looks terrified,' said Colley as the man neared and they could better see his pale features and wide eyes.

'What's wrong, Malcolm?' asked Blizzard.

Watt paused to catch his breath then pointed over at the museum.

'He's dead,' he blurted out.

Having followed him back to the museum, Blizzard and Colley stared at the crumpled body sprawled on the ground before them. Having slipped from the roof the night before, the young man had landed in the lee of the building, obscured from view by a series of large bushes.

'Any idea who he is?' asked Blizzard, glancing round at his sergeant.

'I am pretty sure that his name is Terry Roberts,' replied the detective, crouching down to have a closer look. 'Lifted him last year for nicking lead off a church roof. He lives with his mother on The Spur.'

'And that means,' said Blizzard with a thin smile, 'that we'll have to go on to the estate. Every cloud, eh, lads?'

Marion Roberts sat in the living room of her flat on one of The Spur's upper landings, hunched forward in her chair, hands constantly twisting and untwisted a handkerchief sodden with her tears. A small, thin little woman with mousy brown short hair and pale features, she had been sobbing ever since Blizzard and Colley arrived shortly after lunch. It was a pitiful sight and even the inspector, who usually left the administration of compassion to his sergeant, was moved by her distress. Sitting next to Colley on the sofa, the inspector surveyed the distraught woman for a few moments. He was acutely aware that his well-documented antipathy for The Spur sometimes blinded him to the fact that real people, good people, lived on the estate. It was something that Tommy Rafferty reminded him about from time to time. Rafferty argued that police officers saw so much bad that they forgot how to see the good. Such thoughts ran through the inspector's mind now as he considered how best to approach Terry Roberts's mother.

'Marion,' he said, 'we are truly sorry for your loss but we really do need to find out what happened to Terry.'

The comment brought on a fresh flood of tears and, for a few moments, she was unable to speak. The inspector glanced helplessly at the female constable standing at the door. The young officer came forward and placed a comforting hand on Marion's arm. It seemed to calm her slightly and she looked up at the detectives and nodded.

'I do have to ask why your son was on the museum roof last night,' said Blizzard.

'You can probably guess that.'

Blizzard nodded: he had seen Terry Roberts's record, a litany of thefts, burglaries, handling stolen goods, drunk and disorderly and drug possession. At twenty-three, he was typical of the young men who lived on the estate. His first court appearance had been before the juvenile bench when he was aged just thirteen and he had made regular returns to the magistrates ever since. One of his most recent convictions was for theft, Roberts having been arrested as he and an accomplice left a church in a Transit van loaded with lead stolen from the roof. Terry Roberts had been the first name that ran through the minds of Canham and Robertshaw as they had driven on to the estate two nights previously, having heard the reports of a truck spotted near a church.

'I imagine,' said Blizzard, 'that your Terry was after the lead.'

She shrugged. 'He kept his business to himself.'

'But you did know he had been in trouble before? He was hardly an angel, Marion.'

'How dare you say that,' she said, her eyes flashing anger. 'And with the boy hardly cold.'

'I'm sure he did not mean it that way,' said Colley quickly, glaring at Blizzard and moving to maintain civility. 'But we do have to ask these questions, Mrs Roberts.'

She looked at him for a moment then nodded. There had always been something about Colley that made people trust him. She pointedly turned away from the inspector.

'You ask them then,' she said to Colley.

'We are wondering if there might have been two of them up on the roof, someone with your Terry. A man coming home from the club recalls seeing a man running from the scene shortly after your son fell. Do you know who that might have been?'

Marion shook her head.

'And if you did know, would you tell us?' asked Colley.

She shook her head again. Colley looked at the inspector, who sighed: it was always like this on The Spur. He walked over to the window and stared down over the quadrangle, his eyes scanning the stairwells for signs of another ambush. He would not have been surprised to see something: there had been too many incidents for things to be any other way. And there were plenty of people on The Spur who had never forgiven him for bringing to justice the killers of Kenny Jarvis. Kenny Jarvis, he thought as he stared out of the window. He was always there. The inspector's arrival twenty minutes previously had brought back memories of the days following the PC's death and, as ever when he visited The Spur, there had been something unsettling about the way people had stared silently at him as he crossed the square, something about the way they averted their eyes when he sought to meet their gaze. Some of them would, he knew, dearly love John Blizzard to be the next dead police officer on The Spur. The thought did not worry him. Never had and he imagined it never would.

Blizzard knew he could have sent a couple of junior officers to speak to Terry Roberts's mother but the inspector had refused to brook the idea when Arthur Ronald suggested it after news of Terry Roberts's death filtered back to Abbey Road. There were several reasons why the inspector was determined to go, he had told Ronald, in a hurried discussion in the superintendent's office. Charged atmosphere or not, he wanted to be seen leading from the front, he had said. He wanted the villains to see him, he had said, to realize that the police were taking this seriously, that the chief constable's memo made no difference to the way John Blizzard viewed the estate. Another reason, he had told Ronald, was the strong desire to experience the atmosphere on the estate for himself, to obtain a feel for what was happening. Always a detective who trusted instinct above all other things, John Blizzard was already planning for a raid on The Spur.

Now, from the window of the flat, the chief inspector watched as several youths sauntered across the quadrangle, towards his battered Ford Granada car, which was parked next to the patrol vehicle which had brought the female constable and a uniformed sergeant. There had been much debate about how many officers should accompany the detectives, Ronald arguing for a van-full, Blizzard advocating a low-key approach. Blizzard had won the argument but, low-key or not, there was a police van parked three minutes away from the estate, hidden down a back alley and containing half a dozen officers in full riot gear. Arthur Ronald was not in the mood to take risks, even if Blizzard was.

The inspector watched as the youths approached the police vehicles and the uniformed sergeant got out of the vehicle to confront them. No words were spoken but the sergeant stood, arms folded as he stared hard at them. Blizzard watched as the youths glared back at the uniformed officer then walked on, their mocking laughs reverberating round the deserted quadrangle. Just as Blizzard was moving away from the window, he saw one of the youths turn and spit at the patrol car. Words were exchanged between the sergeant and the youths. Glancing up and seeing the detective watching him, the boy stuck up a single finger, laughed and sauntered away to rejoin his friends.

Blizzard sighed again and let his eyes range around the square, but nothing moved. He knew that the incident would have been watched by many pairs of eyes, though: that was part of the game when you came to The Spur. The inspector turned back into the room.

'Mrs Roberts,' he said, 'our records suggest that your son had a number of known associates from the estate. Is there a chance that he might have been with one of them last night?'

She did not reply.

'We really do need to talk to whoever was with him,' said Colley. 'We need to know why this person did not ring 999, for a start.'

'Would it have saved his life?'

Colley shook his head.

'We think he was dead the minute he hit the ground.'

She nodded. 'I'm glad,' she said. 'Where is he?'

'At the mortuary,' said Colley. 'We will need you to formally identify him, I am afraid. Or perhaps your husband, if you do not feel—'

'Jack died twelve years ago. Cancer. That's when Terry started to go off the rails.' She had a slight smile. 'But thank you for the thought, Sergeant. I'll identify him.'

'We'll take you to the hospital.'

'Thank you.' Marion stood up. 'I'll just ring Barry before we go.'

'Barry?' asked the inspector sharply. 'Who's Barry?'

'Terry's uncle. He's been like a father to him ever since Jack died. Comes over regularly from Sheffield to see him. Used to take him to the football when he was younger.' She looked sadly at the detectives. 'Terry wasn't all bad, you know.'

'No, I'm sure he wasn't,' said Colley.

'He'd even come off the drugs. It would have been five weeks tomorrow. Do you know how much effort it takes to do that in a place like this?'

Blizzard, recalling the signs that her son had still been a user, opened his mouth to comment but closed it when Colley shook his head.

'Such a waste,' said Marion softly, the tears threatening to start again.

'I wonder,' said the sergeant, sensing a softening in her attitude towards the officers, 'if I could ask—'

'No,' she said, tears banished, voice suddenly firm. 'I will not answer any more questions and you'll get no names out of me.'

'But it might help us discover what happened to your son.'

'You know what this place is like, Sergeant.' She gave him a mirthless look. 'Anyone who talks to you might as well start packing their bags now. You've already been here too long.'

Five minutes later, the detectives left the flat, Blizzard and Colley walking ahead of Marion Roberts and the young constable. A group of youths had gathered at the end of the landing, spreading out to block the way to the stairs.

'That's all we need,' murmured Colley, trying to sound calm but mindful of his conversation with Brian Robertshaw the previous day.

'Don't let yourself be provoked,' said Blizzard in a low voice. 'Arthur's last words were that we should avoid any further incidents at all costs. Said he wanted us to be diplomatic.'

'He did know he was talking to you, didn't he?'

Blizzard chuckled and the officers approached the gang, none of whom moved to let them pass. Blizzard gazed into the sullen faces.

'Let us through, boys,' he said.

'Where you taking her?' said one of them, gesturing to Marion. 'What's she been saying?'

'Let us through,' repeated Blizzard.

None of the youths moved.

'Say please,' said the teenager again, leering to display crooked, yellowed teeth. 'I reckon your chief constable would like that. He says you have to be nice to us.'

The others laughed at the joke but fell silent when Blizzard took a step forward and pressed his face into the young man's face, so close he could smell the boy's fetid breath. And smell his fear as well – gang rule or not, everyone on the estate knew John Blizzard.

'If you do not get out of the way,' hissed the inspector, 'I will rip your fucking head off and shit down the hole.'

The youth hesitated.

'And just thank your lucky stars that you caught me on a good day,' continued Blizzard with a disarming smile, 'because if I'd been in a bad mood ...'

He left the words hanging in the air and, after hesitating for a few moments, the youth moved slowly aside and his followers also stepped back, eyeing the officers balefully but not speaking.

'Oh, *that* kind of diplomatic,' said Colley as they clattered down the stairs.

'Well what do you expect?' replied the inspector as they reached the bottom and headed out into the summer sunshine.

The small group headed across the quadrangle, the three officers trying to look relaxed when in fact they were continually scanning the landings for the beginnings of an attack. When they reached the vehicles, the uniformed sergeant greeted their arrival with relief. As Blizzard was getting into his car, one of the youths leaned over the landing balustrade.

'Hey, Blizzard,' he shouted.

The inspector looked up.

'Say hello to Kenny Jarvis for us!' shouted the youth.

'Leave it,' hissed Colley from the passenger seat as the inspector started to walk across the quadrangle.

Blizzard hesitated, glanced up at the grinning youth then back at the sergeant.

'This time I will,' said the inspector, getting back into the vehicle and starting the engines. 'But only this time.'

'Have the police taken to working in bulk?' said the Home Office pathologist Peter Reynolds, staring down at the two bodies on the mortuary slabs.

Blizzard scowled and fumbled in his jacket pocket for the packet of Anadin, his headache having returned on the journey from The Spur to the general hospital's mortuary. Colley, who was leaning against the wall, gave the merest of smiles. Everyone knew the inspector detested Reynolds – a sentiment enthusiastically reciprocated – and their encounters invariably made Blizzard intensely irritable, even without an obstinate hangover. They also made for good sport and Colley always enjoyed regaling colleagues with the details later. His mind went back to moments in the canteen when other officers had surrounded him, demanding a line-by-line account of the men's fractious encounters. This one, thought the sergeant now, would make for good fare and he resolved to remember every word that was spoken.

'Perhaps,' continued Reynolds, fussing round the corpses, 'it is some sort of "buy-one-get-one-free offer"?'

'I hope you were more pleasant when Marion Roberts identified her son,' grunted the inspector, walking over to the sink in search of a glass of water with which to wash down his tablets.

'I was my usual charming self.'

'God help the poor woman,' grunted the inspector.

'I am always charming with the relatives of the dear departed. After all,' and Reynolds gave the inspector a sly look, 'without the sacrifice of their loved ones, I would be out of my remarkably well-paid job. Half million pound mortgages do not pay themselves, you know.'

Blizzard declined to answer so Colley took a few moments to survey the pathologist. The sergeant had never been able to work out Peter Reynolds. He certainly did not come over as likeable and Colley had often wondered if he had any friends at all. He found himself musing now about the pathologist's presumably long-suffering wife. What in earth did she see in him? What was there to see in him? A balding middle-aged little man with piggy eyes gleaming out of a chubby face, and dressed in a shabby, ill-fitting black suit, Reynolds always gave the strong impression that he liked being around death. Revelled in it almost. Colley, whose stomach had long since become inured to the sickly stench of corpses, had never gone as far as to say he enjoyed being in their presence and Blizzard made no secret of his dislike for the experience. Yet Reynolds seemed to love every minute of his job. Colley could never get his head round that.

It was early afternoon and in front of the three men was the naked body of Billy Guthrie, the removal of his clothes having revealed the full extent of the savage beating he had endured. Cuts and livid bruises peppered the body and they could clearly see, now that the blood had been washed off, the extent of the gaping wound on the top of his skull.

Lying next to Guthrie was the body of Terry Roberts, a thin, sallow man with greasy hair, pock-marked skin and sunken eyes. Death could not conceal the fact that he had been unhealthy: running over to his body when it was found behind the museum, Colley had instantly assumed that his skeletal form suggested a heroin user, even before he realized the man's identity. Now, as he surveyed the man's arms, the sergeant could see the series of telltale pinpricks that stood testament to his addiction. Colley shook his head: he had seen it too many times before on mortuary slabs. Far too many times.

Examination of the body also confirmed the officers' conviction that Terry Roberts had fallen from the roof: a section of torn-away guttering lying next to the body at the scene had told the story of his desperate scrabbling in vain for the handhold that would save his life, and now Colley could see that one side of the man's ribcage had caved in on impact with the ground, his left arm was smashed and both legs looked broken. Even to the untrained eye, it was clear what had happened.

Returning from the sink with a glass of water in his hand, Blizzard gazed at the corpses gloomily.

'And?' he said.

'Well, it does not really take an expert to tell you what killed them.'

'Perhaps we can save on your inflated salary then.'

Colley tried to stifle a laugh: he recalled the inspector's fury some weeks earlier when he had discovered how much the pathologist was paid. '*I could buy a team of bloody detectives for that,*' he had exclaimed, and had mentioned it repeatedly in the days that followed, his ire undimmed. Blizzard turned and scowled at his sergeant, who tried to look serious.

'I shall ignore that comment,' said Reynolds. 'Besides, I know you are finding things a bit difficult at the moment. This unfortunate business has all rather ruined your weekend playing trains, has it not, Blizzard? I rather fancied you might bring in that nice PC Hornby to assist you. You'd make a good team.'

Colley failed to suppress the laugh this time.

'Just tell me what killed them,' said the inspector, glowering at the sergeant.

'Oh, please do allow me a little light relief, Blizzard,' said Reynolds. 'After all, I have given up an afternoon playing golf to be here – with your chief constable, actually. A charity match.'

'Not sure I had either of you down as the charitable kind,' muttered Blizzard and nodded at the bodies. 'So what have you found?'

'Let's start with your chap from the signal box, shall we? Our Mister Guthrie. Like I said on the phone, it's all pretty straightforward. As you can see, there is evidence of a large number of blows but my examination suggests that the one that probably killed him was to the top of his head. Fractured his skull.'

'Was a weapon used?'

'I would surmise not. It was a terrible beating, one of the worst I have ever seen. I suspect he may have struck his head on something as he fell.'

'There was a metal fitting near where he fell,' said Colley. 'It had blood on it.'

'Anyway, whatever he hit, I doubt he would have been conscious for long anyway. Had he lived, he would have sustained serious brain damage.'

'Somewhat ironic,' murmured Blizzard.

'Why?'

'It's the way his victims tended to end up. That was certainly the case with Archie Gaines and Denny Rees.'

'Gaines, Gaines – he was a boxer, was he not? And I seem to recall the name Denny Rees as well. A publican in Burniston, I think? Fancy I even did the PM on him.'

'Well, Guthrie did for them both,' nodded Blizzard then looked down at the body. 'There is one thing. Guthrie's ribs. They seem to be sticking out more than you would expect. Was he ill?'

'Well, he's dead if that's what you mean.'

Blizzard glared at the pathologist.

'Sorry, Blizzard,' said Reynolds, thoroughly enjoying himself. 'No, you are, of course, quite right, Billy Guthrie was not a particularly well man. There is evidence that over the past year or so he had been suffering from kidney disease. Its progress seems to have been somewhat rapid.'

'Would it have shortened his life?'

'Not so sure about that but I imagine that he was not far off having to go on regular dialysis. If I had to hazard a cause for the illness, I would suggest that a lifetime of hard drinking did not help.'

'Guthrie was certainly a boozer,' nodded Blizzard. 'They all were, those railmen. And the other guy? What's your official cause of death?'

'Isaac Newton Syndrome.'

'What?'

'Gravity, Chief Inspector.'

Blizzard glowered at the pathologist again.

'As you can see,' continued Reynolds, winking at the sergeant and, as always, giving the distinct impression that he enjoyed winding up the inspector, 'our Mr Roberts has multiple injuries, all of them consistent with a hard impact. Any of them could easily have proved fatal.'

'Did he die immediately?' asked Colley, remembering the mother's questions.

'Undoubtedly.'

'Was he still using drugs?' asked the sergeant. 'Mum reckons he had kicked the habit.'

Reynolds shook his head.

'No chance. Look at his arms; some of those needlepoints are recent. No wonder he fell off the roof – his senses were probably addled.'

'Any chance you can say if he was pushed?' asked Blizzard.

'Pushed?' Reynolds sounded surprised.

'I am wondering if his accomplice shoved him off.'

'Why on earth would he do that?'

Even Colley looked at the inspector with a perplexed expression on his face.

'Who knows?' said Blizzard. 'I just want to know if it is possible.'

'Well, I can't answer that, really,' said Reynolds. 'I am not sure anyone can, Blizzard. The medical evidence in these kind of cases is rarely, if ever, conducive to—'

'But you can't rule it out?'

'Well no, I suppose not, but you know how these things work. You might as well ask me if a purple dinosaur dropped out of the sky and clobbered the poor man to death. I certainly do not want to go on record as indulging in unsubstantiated speculation.'

'I don't need you to go on the record; it's enough that you can't rule it out,' said the inspector, heading for the door. 'Oh, I would appreciate it if you kept the bit about the accomplice possibly pushing him, private. I do not wish it to be relayed to our beloved chief constable at the nineteenth.'

'Well, if he asks, I would have to s—'

'Just keep your trap shut,' snapped Blizzard.

'No, no, no need to thank me,' murmured Reynolds as he watched the inspector stalk from the room. He turned to look at Colley. 'How do you work with him, Sergeant? The man is truly insufferable.'

'Sorry, would love to stay and talk,' grinned Colley, also heading for the door, 'but you heard the inspector, it appears that I've got a purple dinosaur to arrest. And since the babby was born, I just happen to know that he's called Barnie. I reckon that if I look hard enough in Laura's bedroom, I can even come up with a mug shot of the murdering bastard.'

Colley followed the inspector out of the room, chuckling to himself, watched in bemusement by the pathologist.

'Mad,' said Reynolds when the sergeant had gone, 'Absolutely mad, the lot of them. Give me the dead any day. You know where you are with the dead.'

The pathologist looked fondly down at the corpses.

'Eh, boys?'

Once out of the room, Colley discovered that the inspector was already at the end of the corridor and striding out with a new purpose in his step. Colley sprinted to catch him up.

'What was that all about?' asked the sergeant as he fell into step with Blizzard. 'I mean, there is absolutely nothing to indicate that Roberts was pushed. It's an accident, pure and simple. Surely you can see that.'

'Of course I can.'

'Yes, but you said—'

'Think it through,' said Blizzard as he stood aside to let a porter pass with a trolley. 'Our friend lived on The Spur, did he not? The odds are so does his accomplice. Well, until we have proved that Roberts was not pushed, we can describe it as a suspicious death.'

'I would have thought the last thing we wanted on The Spur.'

'Au contraire. It gives us the ammunition to go back on to the estate and turn the whole place over.'

'Ooh, I'm not sure Ronald will go for that,' said the sergeant dubiously.

'It's his idea.'

'What, to base an investigation on something you know to be a load of bollocks?' said the sergeant, raising an eyebrow.

'Well, not exactly that, word for word,' admitted Blizzard as the detectives started walking again. 'But he supports it in broad principle.'

'And am I right to assume that he has not run this "broad principle" past the chief constable?'

'I think it must have slipped his mind. You know how it is,' and Blizzard tapped the side of his head, 'Arthur's getting on a bit.'

'I take it this is one of your little games? I keep telling you that one day you'll get us all sacked.'

'Don't worry, David,' said Blizzard reassuringly. 'I've got official sanction for it.'

'Really?'

'Scout's honour.'

'Game on then,' beamed Colley, as they walked into another corridor. 'Hang on, were you actually ever in the Scouts?'

'Of course not. You know how I hate a uniform.'

Colley was about to reply when the inspector saw a figure walking towards them.

'Hey,' he said, 'isn't that Ramsey?'

The detective inspector walked briskly up to them, a look of excitement on his face and a couple of brown folders clutched in his hand.

'Glad I caught you,' he said.

'For why?' asked Blizzard.

Ramsey looked at the visitors filing past on their way to the wards and gestured for the detectives to step into a deserted side corridor where they would not be overheard.

'For this,' he said in a low voice, holding up one of the folders. 'I think we can say why Terry Roberts was on the museum roof. You were right about him being a heroin addict, Dave, and I am guessing that he was making the money to pay for his drugs by theft. Three convictions in the past twenty-one months. Last one was a factory off Braben Street. Load of copper pipes. Asked for eleven TICs.'

'We know all this,' said Blizzard. 'I'm not sure why you had to come down here to tell us.'

'Ah, but that's not all. See, I did some checking and it seems that Terry Roberts was a known associate of your friend Eddie Gayle.'

'Ok, Chris,' said the inspector, eyes gleaming, 'you've got my undivided attention. How does Gayle fit into this?'

'Well, you know that the rumour is that he part-owns that scrapyard down Elvington Street?'

'Only to fence knock-off stuff. That's why he never goes near the place, in case we catch him at it. His name does not even appear on the company records.'

'Which is exactly the point. See, if Gayle and his cronies are selling things like lead, copper pipework, cabling from railway sidings, through the yard, is it not possible that Roberts and his mates were supplying it?' Ramsey held up the second folder. 'And to make it even more interesting, that is exactly the kind of thing that Billy Guthrie used to do when he was in Hafton.'

'Really?'

'Yeah. It turns out that Guthrie appeared in court eighteen months before he vanished. Two churches and a pub in Burniston and a railway yard in Hafton – over on the east side. Daft really, because he'd worked at the yard. He was sacked after his arrest.'

'At least someone gave evidence against him,' said Blizzard.

'He got unlucky, a passing bobby spotted him.' Ramsey waited for a nurse to walk past. 'Anyway, I was wondering if maybe Guthrie was still into his old racket and had come back to Hafton because of it. What do you think?'

'I think that's excellent work, Chris,' said Blizzard,

patting him on the shoulder. 'Not least because it also links Guthrie to The Spur. No need for purple dinosaurs after all.'

'Purple dinosaurs?' said Ramsey in bemusement.

'I'll tell you later,' replied Colley. 'Look, I hate to piss on your bonfire, Chris, but why would Guthrie come back for a bit of lead off the railway museum roof?'

'Maybe he was after the govnr's train.'

'I keep telling you,' said Blizzard, walking back out into the busy corridor, 'she's a locomotive. They only become trains when they are hooked up to rolling stock.'

'Yes, well whatever you want to call it,' said Ramsey as the officers headed for the front entrance, 'maybe that's what Roberts and his mate were doing on the roof. Casing her out. She's worth a lot of money one way or the other.'

'But how on earth would they get it out of the building?' asked Blizzard.

'I don't reckon they were trying to nick her, guv.'

'Yeah, they'd never get it in the bag,' nodded Colley sagely.

'If we could be serious for a moment,' said Ramsey. 'The Silver Flyer has got lots of valuable metal on her. She'd make for good scrap.'

'Scrap!' exclaimed the inspector in horror.

'It's just a thought. Maybe they were up there casing the place out and planned to come back later.'

'Well, right or not,' said Blizzard as they emerged out into the afternoon sunshine, 'when you put it all together it means that we have a nice excuse to play nice on The Spur. Have ourselves a spectacular.'

As the detectives watched him striding away across the car park, Ramsey looked at Colley and shook his head.

'I sometimes think that guy has got a death wish,' he said. 'He knows what the Chief said yet here he is talking about going on to The Spur, all guns blazing. It's crazy.'

'It is,' nodded Colley. 'But admit it, Chris, don't you just love working with the guy?'

Ramsey watched the sergeant follow his boss across the car park and gave a half-laugh, almost of surprise.

'Damn me if you're not right,' he said.

Ten minutes later, Blizzard and Colley were on their way through the light late afternoon traffic on their way back to the police station.

'Sorry,' said the inspector as he negotiated his way round a stationary bus.

'For what?'

'For wrecking another evening in with Jay and the baby. It's looking like it could be another late one. If I could find a way round—'

'Don't worry. Jay knows how the job works.'

'I know, but these are precious times, David.'

The sergeant looked at him with surprise.

'Is it possible,' he said, 'that John Blizzard might just be going soft in his old age?'

'If you say that when we get back, I will have to kill you. Oh, and less of the old, thank you.'

Before Colley could reply, a voice crackled over the radio.

'Control to DCI Blizzard,' said a woman's voice. 'Message from DS Tulley. The boxing club in Railway Street has opened – he wondered if you wanted to be there?'

'Tell him we're on our way,' said the inspector.

chapter ten

Blizzard pulled the car into a back street a short distance from the city centre. As the detectives got out, the inspector glanced around him. Railway Street stood in what had once been a commercial area full of offices constructed by the city's railway company. When the company ceased to operate in the 1920s, the offices had been taken over by other businesses but Hafton's prolonged post-war economic decline had taken its toll and most of the terraced buildings now stood derelict, their windows boarded up, the doors defaced with obscene graffiti and roofs with gaping holes where the tiles had come off. There was a smell of smoke in the air and Blizzard noticed that one of the houses had recently been burned out, its scorched rafters gaunt and skeletal in the late afternoon sunshine.

'This place was once the commercial heart of the city,' said the inspector, as they started to walk across the street. 'See that building on the corner, the one with the green door? That is where Archibald Galsworthy founded the Hafton Railway Company in 1848.'

'I heard they were going to demolish the whole lot,' said Colley, trying not to look bored. 'I read in the paper that they fancy a bowling alley here.'

'No respect for history,' snorted Blizzard.

'Oh, I dunno, it sounded quite good. Quite fancied taking Laura when she's big enough.'

Blizzard said nothing and together they walked down the street towards Tulley, who had been leaning against a lamppost and watching their conversation with a wry smile. Colley arrived ahead of the inspector and Tulley winked at his colleague.

'You been getting the history lesson then, Dave?' he said quietly.

The sergeant nodded bleakly.

'Hey, you'll like this, guv,' said Tulley in a louder voice, gesturing to a door bearing the words Hafton Railway Boxing Club. 'Apparently the club was set up by the railway company in 1910. There's a plaque on the wall over there.'

'There is indeed,' nodded the inspector. 'This place would have been started when Archibald Galsworthy's grandson was running the company. He was a great sportsman, you know. In fact, I seem to recall that he was a keen boxer. Anyway, is Lawrie Gaines in there?'

'Don't think so. Roly Turner is, mind.'

'How come we have not been able to find him this weekend?' asked the inspector.

'He's been away for a couple of days.'

'Where's he been?' asked Blizzard suspiciously.

'Nothing sinister about it, as far as I can see. There's a poster on one of the windows about a tournament in Scotland. I reckon that's where they've been.'

Blizzard led the way through the door and into a large, if somewhat shabby, gymnasium, with plaster peeling off the walls and several lightbulbs having failed, giving the room a dim appearance with shadows in the corners. Half a dozen teenagers were going through their exercises in a corner, a couple of young men were working at a punchbag and in the ring a couple of fighters in their late twenties were sparring, watched intently by a wiry, white-haired man in his early seventies. He turned to calmly watch their arrival.

'The lads said you were hanging around,' said Turner. 'Reckoned you were Plod. Can I help you?'

'DCI Blizzard,' said the detective, flashing his card. 'I am leading the inquiry into the murder of Billy Guthrie.'

'Yeah, I heard he was dead.'

'How come you know if you have been away?'

'It was on one of the radio bulletins. Besides, doesn't take long for news like that to do the rounds.' Turner glanced at the payphone hanging on the wall. 'We've had half a dozen calls already.'

'From whom?'

'Folks who knew him. Not that I imagine many people will mourn his passing.'

'Why?'

'He was a psycho.'

'A psycho you trained,' said Colley. 'Why do that if you knew what he was like? And why let him loose on a kid like Archie Gaines, for God's sake?'

Turner rubbed his thumb and forefinger together.

'Money,' he said then looked over at the boxers, who had stopped sparring and were listening to the conversation. 'Get back to work!'

They started fighting again.

'Why do you want to talk to me anyway?' asked Turner.

'Because you were in Guthrie's corner the night Archie was injured,' said Blizzard.

'What's that got to do with anything?' said Turner but they noticed that a more cautious look had come into his eyes. 'Surely what happened to the poor lad has nothing to do with the murder of Guthrie. I mean, it must have been twelve years ago now.'

'Actually, we really want to talk to his brother,' said Blizzard. 'Thought you might know where we can find him.'

'Ain't seen Lawrie for ages. Don't look like that, Mr Blizzard, it's the God's honest truth. He ain't really much of a friend.'

'But that's not true, is it?' said Tulley, who had wandered across to a noticeboard where he was examining a series of photographs.

'What do you mean?' Turner sounded guarded again.

The sergeant pointed to a recent picture of Turner and a burly shaven-headed man, arms round each other in what looked like a civic function in a hotel dining room.

'You seem to be pretty friendly here,' said Tulley, peering closely at the picture. 'When was this taken? Looks pretty recent to me.'

'OK,' sighed Turner, 'so I do see Lawrie from time to time. That was the Eastern Counties boxing awards night in Grimsby a few months back.'

'So why lie about it?' asked Blizzard, fixing him with a steely look.

'You know what it's like – didn't want to get myself involved in anything. Never been a great fan of the poliss.'

'Another one,' murmured Blizzard.

'Anyway, so me and Lawrie are friends, there's nowt strange in that.'

'Nothing strange?' asked Colley in astonishment. 'After what your fighter did to his brother? For God's sake, Roly, because of Billy Guthrie, that young lad had no chance, no life! How would you feel if he was your bloody son?'

The other detectives glanced at the sergeant in surprise: such emotional outbursts, once unusual for David Colley, had occurred several times in recent weeks. Turner also looked taken aback by the vehemence of the comments and nodded, his expression suggesting a tone of respect that had not been there before.

'Look,' he said, 'I can understand how you think that. Anyone who's not part of the fight game would struggle to understand it. But Lawrie knew how the game worked, and so did his brother. Anyway, even if Guthrie had not disappeared, I would have dropped him. I'd seen enough. The man was a loose cannon and I felt really bad about what happened to the kid.'

The detectives watched him for a few moments: there was something in his tone of voice that suggested he was telling the truth.

'Anyway,' asked Turner, 'why do you want Lawrie? He'd not seen Guthrie for years. No one had.'

'Well, someone saw him because he's lying in our morgue,' said Blizzard. 'I assume you know that Archie Gaines died three weeks ago?'

'I heard,' nodded Turner. 'Very sad indeed. He was a nice kid.'

'Sad but also interesting.'

'Why?'

'We need to make sure that Lawrie did not take out his grief on Billy Guthrie,' said Blizzard. 'Maybe he heard that Guthrie was coming back to town, decided to settle things once and for all?'

'Lawrie's not like that.'

Noticing that the room had fallen silent and that all the fighters were now listening to the conversation, the coach nodded to a door.

'Can we talk in the office?' he said, then turned to the boxers. 'You lot – get back to work, like I said!'

'If you don't mind, guv,' said Tulley. 'I'll have a word with the lads out here. Maybe some of them know something.'

Blizzard nodded and the other officers followed Roly Turner into the cluttered little office where he made them tea in cracked mugs then sat down behind the desk. He noticed the detectives studying the pictures on the office wall, images of young men clutching trophies.

'Despite what you may think, we do a lot of good, you know,' said Turner, looking at Colley. 'Without us, some of these lads would have ended up in prison.'

'And Archie?' said Blizzard, gesturing to the pictures with his mug. 'Was he like that? Could he have gone bad?'

'Na. He was different. If Guthrie hadn't … well. If he hadn't, Archie could have gone all the way. Such quick hands. That's him in the picture at the end. Next to his brother.'

The detectives looked at the image of a young boxer standing in a ring and holding aloft a trophy as he was surrounded by an excited throng, including a tracksuited Lawrie Gaines. Archie, a willowy, pale man with short, fair hair, eyes ice blue, his face spotted with freckles and a mouth that seemed to be about to break into a smile, somehow exuded a sense of vulnerability. Turner noticed the officers' looks.

'Nothing to look at, was he?' said the coach. 'But I tell you, his appearance was as misleading as they came. By God, could he fight. Reminded me of a young Sugar Ray Leonard. Always dancing round the ring then bang, bang!'

Turner flicked out his fists. 'Lightning quick, he were.'

'So did you coach Archie as well?' asked Colley.

'Just for a few months when he were a kid before I started to concentrate more and more on Billy Guthrie. I know what Guthrie did was unforgivable but in his day he was a brilliant boxer, he really was.' He shook his head. 'What a waste.'

'And Lawrie?' asked Colley, walking over to examine the picture. 'Did he fight?'

'He was different.'

'What does that mean?'

122

Turner hesitated.

'The sergeant asked you a question,' said Blizzard, an edge to his voice. 'Did Lawrie Gaines fight?'

'Not in the ring.'

'Meaning?'

'Meaning that the only fights he got into were ones to protect his kid brother.'

'Did he need to?' asked Blizzard.

'Yes, he did. Archie was a terrific fighter but away from the ring he was meek as anything. Trouble was, some folks fancied their chances against him so Lawrie did the big brother thing. Archie could fight but Lawrie could scrap. There's a difference.'

The detectives exchanged glances.

'I know what you're thinking,' said Turner, 'but that was all years ago. Lawrie was a real hothead then but he's calmed down a lot now. What happened to Archie hit him hard. After it happened, it looked like Archie might not be too bad then he had some kind of stroke or something a few weeks later. That were the end. Changed Lawrie. Changed us all. I know it sounds kind of corny but I think we came to appreciate life a bit more. As far as I know, Lawrie never got into any more scraps. He felt terribly guilty about it.'

'Guilty?'

'Think about it,' said Turner. 'There's Lawrie doing the big brother thing, defending the kid, taking the punches, but where is he when the kid gets mashed up? Standing on the sidelines. Powerless. That never left him. Never left any of us.'

Silence settled on the room. Turner had changed. The unwelcoming front had gone to be replaced by a somehow gentler man, a man who they sensed was struggling with strong emotions. After a few moments, Turner continued talking in a low voice.

'There ain't a day when I do not relive what happened to

that poor kid. He was nothing more than a vegetable at the end, needed everything doing for him. I sometimes used to drive Lawrie over to Nottingham to see him at the home. The home was brilliant, don't get me wrong, them nurses were proper angels, but it was pitiful. Lawrie and Archie would sit there for hours, neither of them saying owt, then we'd come back and Lawrie would be in tears in the car. One time he said it would have been better if the kid had died in that ring.'

'And now he has died,' said Blizzard softly.

Turner nodded.

'Virus or something,' he said, 'You should have seen the funeral. Grown men crying. Big brutes of men with tears pouring down their cheeks. Never seen anything like it. That was the last time I saw Lawrie. He was distraught. Couldn't stop crying. I was pretty upset myself. We all were. Kid was only thirty-one. Such a waste. Fastest hands I ever saw.'

Was it their imagination or did the officers notice a tear glistening in his eyes?

'Exactly what happened that night at the Victoria Hall?' asked Blizzard.

It took three men to carry the lifeless body of Archie Gaines into the dressing room, the young man's head lolling to one side, his eyes having rolled into the top of his head. Frantically, the doctor tried to revive him, watched by a group of concerned officials. Lawrie Gaines burst into the room, the tears starting in his eyes as he watched the desperate battle to revive his kid brother. Gaines turned furiously to Roly Turner.

'How the hell could you let this happen?' he demanded. 'Why didn't you stop him? Throw in the towel?'

'It wasn't meant to happen,' said Turner, almost as if he

could not believe what he was witnessing. 'Honest, Lawrie, it wasn't meant to happen.'

The door opened and in walked a squat man in a sharp black suit. Two burly minders followed him in and all three stood watching the doctor at work.

'Where's Guthrie?' asked the little man, his voice hard-edged.

Turner shrugged.

'Honest, Eddie, I don't know. Last I saw he was running out of the hall.'

'Well, if he's got any sense, he'll keep running,' said Eddie Gayle. 'He just cost me a lot of money.'

Gayle looked at Lawrie Gaines, said nothing and left, followed by his minders.

'What the hell is going on?' asked Lawrie, turning to Roly Turner. 'What does he mean about losing a lot of money?'

Before either of them could reply, Archie Gaines moaned as he started to come round.

'Will he be all right?' asked Lawrie anxiously, rushing over and looking at the doctor.

The doctor shrugged. The door opened again and Lawrie turned to see the figure of a track-suited Billy Guthrie watching the scene but displaying little emotion. One eye was closed and his face still bore the bloodstains from the pounding he had received at the hands of Archie Gaines. Lawrie stared balefully at him: the fighter ignored him.

'Gayle gone?' asked Guthrie, looking at Turner.

'Yeah, he's gone. Only just, mind. He ain't happy with you.'

'Don't suppose he is.' Guthrie nodded at Archie. 'He be OK?'

'What do you think?' exclaimed Lawrie. 'Look at him, just look at him – you proud of what you've done?'

'Should have learned to fight better.'

'He was murdering you!'

Guthrie nodded at Archie, whose eyes had closed again and whose face was deathly white, the breathing shallow.

'Doesn't look like it,' he said.

Lawrie took a step forward, bunching his right fist.

'Leave it, Lawrie,' said Turner, moving quickly to hold out a restraining arm. 'You'll only get yourself into trouble. Besides, you're the least of Billy's worries what with Eddie Gayle after him.'

'What did he say?' asked Guthrie.

'Said you cost him a lot of money. If I were you, I'd keep as far away from Eddie Gayle as possible.'

Guthrie turned to go.

'Archie wasn't supposed to win, was he?' said Lawrie slowly as Guthrie reached the door. 'This wasn't supposed to happen, was it?'

Guthrie turned and shook this head.

'Not this time, son,' he said. 'All the money was on me.'

'But you blew it. They disqualified you.' Lawrie's eyes had a glint of triumph. 'Archie won.'

Guthrie looked down at the prostrate young boxer.

'Did he?' he said quietly and opened the door. 'Did he really?'

And with that he strode out into the corridor.

'So how much did Eddie Gayle put on the fight?' asked Blizzard.

Turner shook his head and the officers could see the fear in his eyes.

'No comment, Mr Blizzard. I've already said too much. And if you want me to put summat down in writing, I ain't going to do it. You know what Eddie Gayle is like.'

'Was that the reason Guthrie disappeared? I mean, Lawrie was right, wasn't he? Guthrie did mess things up. Gayle would not have been very pleased with that. Was that it, Roly? Did he get out before Eddie could get to him?'

'There were lots of reasons why Billy Guthrie skipped town.'

'Like?'

Turner took a sip from his mug of tea.

'I've already talked too much,' he said, 'but if Gayle's heavies were after him – and I ain't saying they were – then I guess that doing a disappearing act would be the best thing to do.'

'Well,' said Blizzard, standing up, 'until we find out what happened, Lawrie is in the frame for murdering Billy Guthrie. If you see him, you tell him that.'

Roly Turner did not reply but his eyes strayed to the picture on the wall of the young boxer, Archie Gaines. Following the train of his gaze, Colley suddenly sat forward and pointed to one of the images showing a teenager being presented with a trophy at what looked like a formal dinner. Something about the face was familiar, less gaunt, less drawn, but unmistakable all the same.

'That's Terry Roberts, isn't it?' he asked.

'Yeah,' nodded Turner. 'How come you know him?'

'Because he died last night. Fell off the railway museum roof.'

'Dear God.' Turner looked genuinely shocked. 'I heard on the radio that someone had fallen, but Terry? Jesus, his poor mum, like she hasn't gone through enough.'

'Was he still a boxer?' asked Colley, walking over to examine the picture.

'Na, dropped out a few years ago. If you ask me, the kid was never the same after his dad passed away. Went off the rails, started getting into trouble. I suspended him a couple of times for bad behaviour so he told me to stick it. Smashed a couple of windows as a goodbye present.'

'Sounds typical,' said Blizzard.

'He weren't a bad lad when I knew him.' Turner glanced at Colley. 'We do try, really we do, but we can't save them all.'

As the two detectives walked back into the gymnasium, Tulley detached himself from a group of boxers and ambled over.

'Anything?' asked Blizzard,

'Not really. A couple of them had heard the rumours that Guthrie was back on Thursday but that's as far as it goes. None of them had seen him for years.'

'When I retire,' said Blizzard, leading the way to the door into the street, 'I am going to open an opticians. I reckon I would do a roaring trade because it seems that no one person in this sodding city ever sees anything.'

He wrenched open the door and walked out into the afternoon sunshine.

'David,' he said, turning back to Colley. 'Did you get the impression that Turner knew more than he was letting on?'

'Very definitely.'

'Not that he'd tell us,' grunted Blizzard and strode across to the car.

'It would seem,' murmured Tulley, watching him go, 'that we've seen the last of the cheery version.'

'Not complaining,' said Colley. 'His cheeriness was really getting on my wick. And maybe now he's got something to moan about, he'll stop banging on about how wonderful railmen are. You'd think they were bloody saints, the way he's been going on about them.'

'My dad was on the railways,' said Tulley.

'Yeah, well, I'm sure he was a nice man.'

'Na,' grinned Tulley, 'he was an old git. Talking of old gits – have you noticed how Blizzard keeps on talking about what he's going to do when he retires?'

'I had, actually.'

'Jesus,' and Tulley's face assumed an appalled expression, 'imagine what he'll be like as a pensioner.'

'Don't,' said Colley, wagging a finger at him. 'Just don't.'

*

The detectives had been gone an hour when the three men entered the gymnasium. Everyone fell silent as Eddie Gayle and his two minders walked across the floor towards Roly Turner, who had been supervising a training bout in the ring. Fat, short and perspiring in the clammy early evening heat, Gayle was aged in his mid forties, thinning black hair covered by a poorly fitting wig, and dressed as ever in a sharp dark suit which would have looked good on anyone else. His companions were large men, barrel-chested, shaven-headed. Turner eyed them all nervously.

'Eddie,' he said, trying to sound calm, 'what brings you here?'

'I hear my good friend Mr Blizzard has been to see you. Him and his muppets.'

'Who told you that?' asked Turner, glancing accusingly at the silent boxers.

'That is not relevant. What is relevant is our friend Mr Blizzard and what he was asking you about.'

'I told him nothing.'

'Told him nothing about what?'

Turner hesitated.

'Told him nothing about what, Roly?' rasped Gayle and one of his heavies took a step forward.

'He were asking about Archie Gaines,' said Turner quickly. 'He seemed to know everything.'

'And how,' said Gayle quietly, 'would he know that?'

chapter eleven

The summer evening shadows were starting to fall over the city when Colley edged his car out of the Abbey Road car park. Waiting to let a taxi past, he glanced in the rear-view mirror and saw the expressionless features of Megan Rees staring back at him. He gave a slight shudder: that stare again, it seemed to go right through him. Turning round, he saw that Fee Ellis, sitting in the other rear seat, was looking out of the window, wrapped up in her own thoughts. She noticed him looking at her and gave a slight smile. Megan Rees said nothing.

Colley pulled out into the light early evening traffic and started heading west through the suburbs. It was a journey that would take him away from the areas that provided the detectives with most of their daily tasks, areas which had brought them so many times into the criminal arc of men like Eddie Gayle. However, as the division stretched towards the western fringes of the city, taking the route along which the sergeant was driving, the neighbourhoods changed dramatically. Colley steered the car through wide tree-lined roads lined with huge mock-Georgian houses hidden behind high walls and hedges. Some of the houses, many of which were ivy-covered and several of which had outdoor swimming pools, were owned by business executives from the aviation plant in the city, others by self-made entrepreneurs and highly paid council executives. And some, Colley knew, were owned by villains. For the division's detectives, such a contrast had always proved intriguing.

Ironically, the leafy suburbs brought the officers back into Gayle's orbit. It was into one such road that Colley now turned, taking the car between two rows of trees, the setting sun dappling its way through the overhanging boughs. Glancing to his right, he gave a thin smile: he knew that the first house he saw, the one with the high wall and the gates with the huge ornate lions, belonged to Gayle. One day, thought the sergeant as he drove past the house and glanced at the new Jaguars parked on the drive, one day we will come for you, my lad. Maybe, he thought, as he continued along the road, that day was nearer than everyone believed. Blizzard certainly seemed to think so.

Returning his attention to the road, the sergeant turned into another road then down a cul-de-sac where he noticed a sign which read *The Oaks* and was adorned with a nice drawing of a house and a spreading tree. All very idyllic, thought the sergeant, except that the small logo in the corner of the sign gave away its real purpose. *NHS*, it said. Colley steered the vehicle off the road to be confronted with a set of closed wrought iron gates.

'It looks like a prison,' said Megan as the car pulled to a halt, the first time she had spoken in the journey.

'I'm sure it's not that bad,' replied Fee.

'I don't deserve this. I didn't kill Billy Guthrie, you know.'

Fee did not reply and, having brought the car to a halt, Colley turned in his seat to stare at Megan.

'Care to elaborate on that?' he asked.

'What's to elaborate? I didn't kill him. How can you elaborate on something that did not happen? Your Mr Blizzard knows I didn't kill him. Blizzard will get me out of here.'

'I wouldn't hold out much hope,' said Colley. 'He's not exactly famed for his services to mental health. Do you know who did kill Billy Guthrie?'

Megan Rees said nothing.

'If you do, it might help you.'

Again, Megan Rees said nothing and the detective turned back to wind down his window and talk into the intercom on the wall.

'Detective Sergeant David Colley,' he said. 'Mrs Randolph is expecting us – we have a guest for you.'

'Guest!' snorted Megan Rees.

'That's what they like to call you,' said Colley, as the gates swung open and the car edged up the winding drive towards the large double-fronted house. 'I am sure they will look after you, Megan.'

'It's still a loony bin!' she sneered.

'I believe it's what they call an Intermediate Assessment Unit,' said Colley, pulling up outside the house, switching off the engine and getting out of the car to open the rear door.

'It's a loony bin!' snapped Megan, getting out. 'No amount of fancy words can hide that. And there is no way I should be here.'

'The psychiatrist believes they need to take a closer look at you,' said the sergeant calmly.

'That man!' exclaimed Megan. 'He was another one who only wanted to get into my knickers. And I could smell the drink on his breath.'

'I really do not—'

'Have you ever been in one of these places?' asked Megan as the three of them walked up the front steps.

'No,' said Colley, adding innocently, 'have you?'

'Don't play games, Sergeant, you know I have. Another damned fool shrink sent me to one of these places after my mother died. Before they sent me to that horrible foster home. Said I needed help expressing my grief. Is anyone feeding my dog?'

The sudden change in subject matter caught the sergeant by surprise.

'Well?' she repeated, fixing him with a demanding stare. 'Is anyone feeding my dog?'

'Er, yes, I believe he has been taken to the pound.'

'Pound?' She looked furiously at him. 'You let them take him to that filthy place? You're a dog owner; would you let them take your dog there?'

'How do you know that I have a dog?' asked Colley quickly.

Fee Ellis looked at the sergeant in surprise: she had met the dog enough times on evenings at his house. They had often laughed about it because Blizzard detested and feared dogs above all else. Whenever they went round, the chief inspector had insisted that the German Shepherd, a failed police dog, had to be kept in the downstairs utility room. Attempts by Jay and Colley to introduce Blizzard to the animal had failed, with plenty of growling – on both sides. Once locked away, the animal would bark from time to time to remind the inspector that he was there. Blizzard's nervous expression had seemed funny then: not now.

'Well,' said the sergeant. 'How do you know that?'

Megan said nothing but allowed herself an expression of satisfaction when she saw the troubled look on both detectives' faces. The sergeant was about to say something else when a smartly dressed middle-aged woman appeared from an office and walked briskly towards them, her heels clicking on the tiled floor.

'Sergeant Colley,' she said extending a hand. 'Myra Randolph. I am the manager here.'

She turned to the two women, looking first at Fee Ellis

then at Megan Rees. Confusion flitted momentarily across her face.

'Yes,' said Megan with a slight smile, 'it can be difficult to tell the nutters apart from the rest of the world, can't it, Mrs Randolph?'

Blizzard was still in his office when Colley returned. The sergeant slumped wearily into a chair.

'How's Megan?' asked the inspector.

'Can't work her out.'

'Do you fancy her?'

'Don't you start.'

'Sorry,' said Blizzard, who was aware that Colley had been teased by fellow officers about the way Megan seemed to have taken a shine to the sergeant at the railway siding. 'Bad phraseology. I mean do you fancy her for Guthrie?'

Colley shook his head.

'Why?'

'Instinct – and the fact that there's no way a slip of a girl like that could do that to him.'

'Unless she had help.'

'Like who?' asked the sergeant. 'From what we can see, all she has are a few friends on the college art class she attends and that's it. They're more likely to draw his portrait than murder him. Mind, there is definitely something strange about her. She knew I had a dog. How would she know that? Do you think she has been stalking me or something?'

'Probably just a lucky guess.'

'Maybe,' said Colley but he did not sound convinced.

'So who do we fancy, then?' asked Blizzard.

'I'd love to say Eddie Gayle but he doesn't make mistakes that easily.'

'Maybe he did this time. Anyway, if we assume he didn't, what about Lawrie Gaines?'

'A better bet,' nodded Colley. 'Motive, opportunity and now he's missing. Ticks all the boxes.'

The sergeant yawned and Blizzard glanced up at the clock. It said 8.45.

'Get yourself home,' said the inspector. 'See that baby of yours.'

'She'll be asleep. Always sleeps between six and midnight, then gets up for a bit to play.'

'Then see Jay. Crack open a bottle of wine.'

'Hell no!' exclaimed Colley. 'That's how we got Laura!'

Blizzard chuckled.

'Besides,' said the sergeant, 'I've got those reports to fin—'

'Go home. That's an order.'

Colley's face broke into a grin and he stood up.

'Maybe I will,' he said. 'Besides, if I recall correctly, they have started showing Petrocelli. Wonder if he's finished that bungalow yet? He's been on it longer than you were building that bleeding train.'

'Locomotive.'

Colley laughed and headed for the door. 'See you in the morning.'

'Yeah. Good night, David.'

The inspector listened as the sergeant's footsteps echoed down the empty corridor. He sat in silence for a few moments then Fee put her head round the door.

'You finished?' she said.

'No,' said Blizzard, standing up and unhooking his jacket from the back of his chair, 'I've got one more thing to do.'

'Well, don't be long. I'm going to get a nice bottle of reddo on the way home. That sound good?'

'Certainly not,' said Blizzard. 'I've just discovered what happens when you drink it.'

*

Joe Hargreaves sat amid the deepening evening shadows of his living room and stared down at the black-and-white photograph of two men in overalls and railmen's caps, smiling as they straddled a locomotive. He had been gazing at the image for the best part of an hour. It had been taken in one of the sheds at the locomotive works in the late 1940s when he and his brother were both young men. Joe had not taken out the album for many years but the death of Billy Guthrie had brought back so many memories and, sitting there as darkness settled silently around him, he had given up to the overwhelming tide of words, snatches of conversation, images and feelings that jostled for his attention as he let the past play like a showreel. Then came sounds, the clanging of tools, the holler of men – and a sensation, the weedling chill of the early morning air in the great shed as the men turned up for work on winter mornings.

Looking at the smiling faces, Joe sighed softly. Carefree days, he thought. Days with so much hope – and for what? Matty long gone and he himself a sad and lonely widower crippled by lung disease and arthritis and hardly able to leave the house. He felt the tears welling deep within. His reverie was disturbed by a knock on the front door. He glanced up at the clock: 8.45 it said. Walking with some difficulty – sitting for long periods of time always made his joints stiffen up – he made his way down the gloomy hallway and tentatively – Joe Hargreaves had few visitors – opened the door into the street.

'Roly,' he said. 'Long time, no see.'

'I had to come. I think it's time we had a talk.'

'I think you are probably right.' Hargreaves gestured inside. 'I'll put the kettle on.'

*

'Come on, Steve,' said Blizzard, unable to conceal the frustration in his voice. 'I really do need your help. If there's a chance I can bring in Eddie Gayle then I really need to get some more—'

'I should have kept my trap closed last night,' said McGarrity flatly. 'I was drunk.'

Dusk had fallen over Hafton and the two men were sitting, cradling cans of lager, at the kitchen table in McGarrity's terraced house. The councillor had lived for thirty-five years in the area close to Tenby Street railway station. There had been a time when it seemed that the house would succumb to the bulldozers, his street listed among those earmarked for the city council's demolition programme. However, at the last moment, the architects had altered the scheme and McGarrity's home had survived. McGarrity had always been evasive when questioned about the late stay of execution, his only response an enigmatic smile.

Normally, Blizzard's Sunday night visits to see his old friend were pleasant occasions, the two men yarning endlessly about the golden age of steam, but this time there was tension in the air. It started with Blizzard's unannounced arrival: McGarrity had appeared nervous and reluctant to let him in. Ever since he had arrived, Blizzard had noted his friend's unwillingness to talk about the events surrounding Guthrie's death and now, as the last rays of the summer sun streaked the evening sky, the inspector decided to try one last time.

'Look,' he said, 'I can understand that you are unwilling to—'

'I've told you all I can.'

'I don't believe that.'

'Well, it's the truth, John.'

Blizzard took a sip of his lager and eyed his friend for a few moments.

'Come on, Steve,' he said, his voice more conciliatory 'it was you that pointed me in Gayle's direction in the first place. Remember?'

'I said you should look at Lawrie Gaines, John. I never said you should look at Eddie Gayle. Jesus, man, you know what happens to people who cross him. If word gets out that I said anything, you'll be looking for me in the canal.'

'Don't worry. I said I'd keep you out of this.'

'Don't worry! That's easy for you to say but you know the truth, John. Nobody is kept out of it when Eddie Gayle is concerned. I'm sitting here dreading the knock on the door.'

Both men started when the doorbell rang.

'Jesus Christ,' gasped McGarrity then suddenly relaxed. 'No, actually that will be Tommy.'

'What's he doing here?'

'He said he might pop round for a drink,' said McGarrity, getting up. 'But I tell you now, John, he'll react the same way I did when you said you wanted Gayle.'

As McGarrity headed out into the hallway, Blizzard walked out of the back door and out into the yard. A sultry stillness had settled over the night, an oppressive heaviness that seemed to dampen sound: the noise of the traffic on the bypass seemed strangely dulled. The inspector stared out into the neatly kept yard with its colourful pots of flowers, the blooms trailing their way along the red-brick wall. Down at the far end, disappearing into the gathering darkness, stood a small outhouse with a yellow door, in front of which was a wooden trellis archway trailed with a climbing rose, the fragrance pungent in the night air. Blizzard had never been a big fan of gardening but he knew it was a big passion for McGarrity and that the flowers had been lovingly nurtured by his friend. The inspector took another sip of his lager and sighed: this was no place for harsh words between friends. This should have been a pleasant experience but talk of Eddie Gayle had sent his mind racing. And Blizzard knew he had been pushing everyone hard on the subject.

Listening to the hushed conversation in the hallway, but unable to make out the words although he did think he detected a third voice, Blizzard allowed his mind to roam to his enmity with Eddie Gayle. Gayle was well known to the police, a man who stalked the darker areas of the city, spreading his own brand of fear and hatred. And yet he had proved, so far at least, an 'untouchable' for the police even though Blizzard and his detectives had been after him for years. Gayle's ability to talk his way out of the very tightest of spots, aided by his slippery lawyer, had long been a source of growing infuriation for Blizzard.

Gayle's 'legitimate' business was property. Preferring to present himself to the public as a man of great standing within the community, he was the owner of many of the city's beautiful Victorian houses in the streets that fanned out from the city centre. He liked to claim that he was helping to ease Hafton's acute accommodation crisis whilst also preserving precious old properties, but everyone knew they were just words. Eddie Gayle's real business was about making money whatever the cost to other people, and had been for years. Behind what little respectability his flash motors and cheap suits afforded him, Gayle was a crook and a thug. He spent little money on his houses and, despite the extortionate rents he charged for the rooms, most of them were pits of squalor with damp walls, curling wallpaper, tatty carpets and rickety furniture. And they were freezing in winter, Gayle having refused to invest in central heating systems for his tenants, a mix of DSS clients, drop-outs and impecunious students. Those who complained or fell behind on the rent received a visit from Gayle's enforcers. And warning letters to Gayle from council officers went unheeded. Actions that went unactioned. There had even been rumours of Gayle and his heavies turning up at a housing officer's house one night but the official had declined to confirm them when approached by the police. Eddie Gayle had always exerted a stranglehold over those whose testimony could send him to jail.

Blizzard knew why people were scared of Gayle, knew that there was more to him than a few bedsits, knew that he controlled an empire whose activities took in everything from drug trafficking and cigarette smuggling to money laundering and a protection racket for the city's nightspots, all of it ruthlessly enforced by his henchmen. But whenever the detectives sensed that they were getting close to Gayle, witnesses seemed to melt away. Several had disappeared altogether and all police efforts to trace them had failed. Murdered? No one knew.

Hearing the men walking along the hallway, Blizzard returned to the kitchen and awaited their arrival. He was not surprised to see the third man with them when they walked into the kitchen. He knew the others were good friends with George Haywood. When Blizzard had seen him at the railwaymen's dinner the night before, Haywood had been wearing a suit; now he was attired in a more casual manner in a pale-blue shirt and a pair of brown trousers. He shared the nervous expressions of the others, each of them eyeing him with looks which made it clear that they would rather he was not there.

'What you here for?' asked Rafferty bluntly.

'Just a social visit, Tommy.'

'Why don't I believe that?' said Rafferty, accepting the proffered can of lager from McGarrity and sitting down heavily in a chair at the table.

He took a few seconds to recapture his breath then cracked open the can. Haywood took a beer out of the fridge and leaned against the cooker. He seemed ill at ease.

'Look,' said Blizzard, 'I know this is difficult for you. For all of you.'

'Too true it is,' said Rafferty.

'Where you been tonight then?' Blizzard tried to strike a more conciliatory tone: the prickly atmosphere was not conducive to obtaining information.

'Down the Club.' Rafferty nodded at George Haywood. 'Been toasting the Old Lady's health.'

'My head would seem to suggest that we did enough of that last night,' said Blizzard ruefully.

The others laughed and the atmosphere relaxed slightly.

'So why *are* you here?' asked Haywood.

'Getting nowhere with my investigation. Need help.'

'Look,' said Rafferty, glancing at the others, 'I told you, we don't want to get involved.'

'Yeah, Eddie Gayle does that to people,' said Blizzard. 'Roly Turner was the same.'

'Not surprised,' said Rafferty.

'You know him?'

'Used to work with him when we were on the railways,' said Rafferty. 'Even did a bit of coaching for him down the club when I were younger.'

'And did Eddie Gayle ever—?'

'I ain't talking about him,' said Rafferty quickly, taking a swig of his drink. 'Besides, it's not just Eddie Gayle that's causing the problems. Look at it from my point of view. I heard you were on the estate seeing Terry Roberts's mum. People always get funny when you turn up. People know that we are friends.'

'That's why I asked to meet here. Make it easier for you.'

'Why is CID involved anyway?' asked McGarrity. 'I thought it was an accident that the lad fell off the roof.'

'We reckon Terry Roberts was on the roof in the furtherance of crime.'

'Furtherance of crime? That what they call it?' Rafferty gave a low laugh. 'Besides, why would someone from The Spur be into crime?'

'You are right, it does sound ridiculous now you say it,' said Blizzard and allowed himself a smile.

'I still don't see why you would be interested in that,' said McGarrity. 'I didn't think that chief inspectors did that kind of thing. I thought you left it to lowly constables.'

'There may be a link between Gayle and Terry's death. Look, all I'm asking is—'

'Right, that's it, I'm going,' said Rafferty, getting to his feet.

'I'll go with you,' said Haywood, placing his can on the worktop. 'No way I want to be involved in anything like this.'

'No, no,' said Blizzard, also standing up and gesturing for him to sit back down. 'I should be the one to go. Just think about what I said, though, will you?'

'And you think about us,' said McGarrity. 'We're just ordinary blokes, John. Just ordinary blokes. And it ain't fair to put us in this position.'

As Blizzard walked out into the hallway, he sighed to himself: like he always said, Eddie Gayle did that to people.

After the inspector had gone, the three men sat drinking long into the night, their conversation urgent and hushed. They tried to look relaxed when McGarrity's wife came in from the bingo but she realized immediately that something was wrong. Not that any of them would admit it. They did not need to: Margaret McGarrity had known for several days that something was troubling her husband: she could see the fear in his eyes. And Rafferty, he had been different, edgy, snappy. Not like his usual self. George Haywood she did not really know but he also seemed on edge as he sat at the kitchen table. She noticed how he refused to meet her gaze.

After bidding them good night, Margaret walked slowly up the stairs to bed but found herself unable to sleep, conscious only of the low murmur of conversation down in the kitchen. Finally she did drift off but was jerked awake when the phone rang, its shrill tones cutting through her disturbed dreams. Sitting up in bed, she realized that McGarrity was still downstairs. Reaching over to the bedside clock, she saw that it was after two in the morning. Padding quietly along the landing, she paused at the top of the stairs and stared down at her husband, who was standing by the little table in the hallway, listening to the voice on the other end of the line.

'Just you keep your mouth shut,' her husband hissed.

Margaret McGarrity could not catch the reply – the person on the other end seemed to be speaking in a low voice – but whatever was said it frightened her husband. Slowly he put the receiver down and walked back into the kitchen, the walk of a man who seemed to have aged before her eyes. He did not look up.

chapter twelve

'Are you sure about this?' asked Ronald. 'I mean, really sure? Megan Rees is our main suspect, for God's sake, and you want to let her go. Think of the flak that will fly if you are wrong.'

'I'll add it to the rest,' said Blizzard.

It was shortly after three on Monday afternoon and the two officers were sitting in the superintendent's office, cradling their customary mugs of tea, the inspector having returned to the station a few minutes previously. After a day of largely fruitless inquiries, which had darkened Blizzard's mood and led to irritable confrontations with a number of colleagues, the inspector had taken himself off to one of his favourite places, a place where his mind could find the calm it so often craved amidst the activity of a murder inquiry. Blizzard had long found himself drawn to the River Haft running through the city, beguiled by the gentle lapping of its waters, and had felt his mind settling the moment he parked his car and walked down the foreshore, the gravel crunching underfoot. He had, in his time, spent many long hours sitting and watching as the huge tankers plied their trade, bound for the chemical complex on the southern bank of the Haft.

However, there was more to river watching for the chief inspector: everyone knew that when Blizzard's mind settled, crimes were solved. On this occasion, he arrived shortly after two and stood on the foreshore for a few minutes before walking for several hundred yards along the pebble-strewn beach. From time to time, he would stop to stare further along the bank, in the direction of the city centre, to where skeletal cranes and ramshackle old sheds stood testament to shipyards that had long since died. He had always assumed that his connection with the river was something to do with his passion for industrial history and the Haft's role in the city's rapid expansion in the 1800s.

As Blizzard stood and watched, a small pleasure boat cruised past, heading for the city's new marina, early evidence of the river's regeneration. As Blizzard took in all these sights, his mind turned the case over and over. Time and time again, he came back to Lawrie Gaines, the man with the clearest motive to kill Billy Guthrie. The death of his brother three weeks previously had, according to neighbours interviewed by Blizzard's detectives, upset him deeply and they had spoken of a barely concealed fury when he talked about the events that night in the boxing ring. Lawrie Gaines had, the people said, a burning hatred of Billy Guthrie. It was, Tulley and Fee had both said, as if something had changed in Lawrie Gaines when his brother passed away. Friends and neighbours had seen a man saddened by the ways of the world, but nevertheless coming to accept them, transformed into one railing against its injustices. And John Blizzard had seen enough people sharing the same sensation end up in courtrooms to take such considerations anything but seriously. Walking back in the direction of the car, Blizzard had come to his decision. Now, having voiced his thoughts, the inspector could see that it had not gone well, Ronald's expression one of doubt.

'I mean, why would you want to release Megan Rees at this stage of the inquiry?' asked the superintendent. 'Surely she must be one of your main suspects? She's got a record of mental instability, you yourself said that she is a very angry and disturbed young woman, and what's more, she's got a strong motive. And don't forget that she did find the body and you know as well as I do that the statistics say that the person who—'

'I know all that but there's nothing to link Megan Rees to the death of Billy Guthrie. It's wrong to keep her in.'

'But the credit card that Ross found on the wasteland?'

'I am sure it was a plant. And a crude attempt at that.'

'By whom?'

'Not sure yet. Look, Arthur, I just do not think she is the murderer.'

'But the psychiatrist—'

'Pish,' exclaimed Blizzard, his antipathy to anyone with an 'ist' at the end of their job title well known throughout Abbey Road. 'That girl is as sane as you or me.'

Ronald looked at him dubiously.

'Come on, Arthur, level with me. If she wasn't in that unit, what would we have to hold her on? Give me one shred of evidence that would stand up in court if we had to appeal for an extension? OK, so she's a bit tapped but there's not a magistrate in the land would make a decision based on that. Half the magistrates in this city are a sandwich short of a picnic anyway.'

Ronald did not reply.

'I asked Chris Ramsey the same question,' continued Blizzard. 'Thought I would see what the voice of the moral majority had to say for itself, and he could not give me an answer either. I ran it past Ross as well and he said the same thing and, as for Colley, he reckons—'

'Thanks for coming to me first,' said the superintendent acerbically. 'I assume you had a word with the cleaner as well?'

'Yeah, but she started talking about the social cohesion of

post-war mental health legislation while shoving Domestos down the toilets so I left her to it. Sorry, Arthur, but I wanted to try it out on other people before I brought it to you. Get my ducks in a row, as those senior officers incapable of independent thought would say.'

Ronald gave him a pained look.

'Look,' said the inspector, 'the only link to Billy Guthrie is that he killed her father.'

'Not sure I can think of many stronger motives.'

'Agreed, but I keep coming back time and time again to the fact that there is nothing to link her with the attack. No forensics, nothing. Unless you can think of something, I cannot see an alternative to letting Megan Rees go. Unless you have any bright ideas.'

Reluctantly, Ronald shook his head.

'In which case, can you talk to the shrink and get her out of there? Let's be honest, you did lean on him a bit to put her there in the first place so we could have a bit more time.'

'It's all rather irregular,' said Ronald unhappily. 'He wasn't exactly delighted to be involved in the first place. Look, why can't we leave her in there and let things run their course? She'll get out eventually anyway.'

'I am sure she will,' said Blizzard downing his tea and standing up, 'but I really do not want to wait much longer. I mean, how the hell can we keep her under surveillance if she's stuck in a padded cell trying to persuade some doctor that she's not Napoleon Bonaparte?'

Ronald watched his friend stride out into the corridor.

'Now that's my boy,' he beamed, then his face clouded over and he shouted after the inspector. 'Hang on, does that mean you think she killed him or not?'

'Yes,' said the inspector's disembodied voice.

*

It was just after six when Blizzard and Colley got out of the inspector's car and walked up the steps to The Oaks, to be met by the unsmiling figure of Mrs Randolph.

'I have to say that this is most irregular,' she said tartly, ignoring the officer's proffered hand.

'Strangely enough,' said the inspector as they walked into the hallway, 'that was the word used by my superintendent.'

'Yes, well in my view, both of you need to learn more respect for the ways of the NHS. Normally, people tend to stay with us for longer than this in order that a full assessment can be conducted.'

'Hey, don't blame me,' said Blizzard innocently. 'Blame the shrink.'

'The *psychiatrist*,' said Mrs Randolph angrily, 'expressed similar reservations to mine. He feels that she really should be kept here until she has undergone a thorough—'

'Look, Mrs Randolph,' said Blizzard, giving her one of his stares and noting disconcertedly that it appeared to have little effect, 'I really do not have time for all this. If you want to take it further, talk to my superintendent, Arthur Ronald. Nice man; you'll like him.'

'Your superintendent,' replied Mrs Randolph coldly, 'was the one that seems to have suggested that the psychiatrist recommend her release. He was most insistent.'

'There you are,' beamed Blizzard. 'I said it was nothing to do with me.'

Colley smiled slightly: Blizzard had always detested officious people and, in the sergeant's view, there were few more satisfying sights than watching the chief inspector dealing with them. A door to their left opened and one of the nurses led out Megan Rees, who stared calmly at the detectives.

'I told you I was not mad,' she said.

'The ways of the medical world,' said the inspector with a

shrug. 'They're a mystery to me as well, Megan. Anyway, you are free to go now. We'll drive you home.'

'I have ordered a taxi.'

'For why?'

'I've had enough of police cars,' said Megan and with a hard stare at Mrs Randolph, she walked out of the building and down the gravel path.

Hearing the sound of a car's horn in the street, she quickened her stride. The detectives stood at the top of the steps and watched her in silence. As the gates opened, she turned.

'Oh, and Mr Blizzard?' she shouted.

'Yes?'

'Don't think of getting someone to tail me,' and she gave a crooked smile. 'I'll only spot them.'

'And what exactly,' murmured Colley to the scowling inspector, 'have you got in mind for plan B?'

'I take it everything is in place?'

'Yeah, we've got a car round the corner, but let's hope that she is not as good as her word. She does seem to be pretty clued up.'

'I blame television,' said Blizzard. 'They all think they're bloody detectives now.'

'Yeah, Laura's learning loads from Cagney and Lacey.'

The gates swung slowly open and Megan Rees disappeared from view. Both officers wondered if they would ever see her again. It was as the detectives were getting into their car that the radio crackled into life.

'Message for DCI Blizzard,' said a man's voice. 'Lawrence Gaines has been spotted.'

'Where?' asked the inspector quickly.

'One of our traffic patrols saw him on the Docks Road. He's on foot and carrying a suitcase.'

'OK, can you tell them to meet us there,' said Blizzard,

switching on the engine. 'Oh, and can someone ring the Port Police and square it for us to go on to their patch, please? We don't a repeat of the debacle from last time. We couldn't move for people spitting their dummies out.'

'Will do, sir,' said the man and the line went quiet.

'Now where on earth,' said Blizzard, glancing at his sergeant as the inspector guided the car down the drive, 'would our Mr Gaines be going at a time like this?'

'Maybe he fancied a holiday,' said Colley, reaching into his suit jacket pocket and fishing out his mobile phone. 'I know how he feels. Talking of which, better ring home.'

'When this is over,' said the inspector as the car edged into the road, 'you are going to take all those lieu days. Tell Jay I said that, will you? Tell her I said that you need to look after yourself now you're a dad.'

'Do you know,' said the sergeant, dialling the numbers, 'you are starting to sound like my mother. Or, as I like to call her, the babysitter.'

Within twenty minutes, the detectives had arrived at the city's terminal, the inspector parking the Granada in the private car park used by the Port Police. Ushered up to the control tower by one of the Port Officers, he and Colley stood and surveyed the scene stretching out in front of them. The quayside was virtually deserted, the tarmac glistening from the drizzle that had started to die out as the early evening sun broke through the cloud again. Staring out of the window, the inspector could see a large ferry docked at one of the main berths: he assumed the vessel was bound for one of the Dutch ports. Beyond the ferry stretched the dark waters of the Haft, the surface peppered with the raindrops that had suddenly started to fall harder. A rainbow started to form over the far bank: it had been like this all summer.

'There they are,' said the Port Officer, pointing to a line of people emerging from below the tower, clutching suitcases and holdalls. 'They'll be heading for Entrance Number 2.'

The officer handed Blizzard a pair of binoculars and the inspector scanned the people now snaking across the tarmac.

'Fourth from the back,' he said, passing the glasses to Colley.

Colley stared down at the burly shaven-headed man in the jeans and black leather jacket. The man carried a suitcase and had a knapsack slung over his shoulder.

'Yeah, I reckon that's him,' nodded the sergeant.

'So how do you want to play it?' asked the Port Officer. 'I can't delay the departure of the ferry, I am afraid. It's already running fifteen minutes late.'

'No need to,' said Blizzard. 'Let's lift him now. I've got a couple of uniforms on the gate in case he makes a break for it.'

'I've got a couple of bodies at the barriers as well,' said the officer leading the detectives down the gloomy stairwell and pushing his way out on to the tarmac. 'Between us, we should catch chummy.'

Once they were out, the officer led the detectives towards the line of passengers.

'Lawrence Gaines!' shouted Blizzard.

Gaines whirled round and gave a cry of alarm. Before any of the officers could react, he had started to run, hurling away his suitcase and barging past startled passengers as he sprinted towards the exit gate. Colley gave chase, the sergeant covering the ground rapidly to hurl himself into a rugby tackle, grabbing hold of the fleeing man's legs and sending him crashing to the ground. Gaines lay winded for a moment then lashed out with his right boot, catching the sergeant in the stomach. Colley groaned and staggered backwards. Gaines leapt to his feet and advanced on the detective, fist raised. Colley, temporarily winded, held up an arm to protect himself.

'I wouldn't do that, Lawrie,' said Blizzard, running up and trying not to breathe too heavily. 'You are in enough trouble as it is.'

'I ain't done nothing,' said Gaines, lowering his hand.

'There's folks as might think otherwise. And I tend to be a little suspicious of suspects who try to run for it.'

All the fire went out of Gaines and he shook his head in defeat and reached down to the sergeant. Colley flinched but Gaines offered him a helping hand to his feet.

'Sorry, mate,' said Gaines as the sergeant rubbed his sore stomach. 'I panicked.'

Colley looked ruefully at him then produced a pair of handcuffs from his pocket.

'They won't be needed,' said Gaines. 'You'll get no trouble from me. Time to finish this nonsense once and for all.'

A s Lawrie Gaines sat opposite the two officers in the interview room at Abbey Road later that evening, his demeanour retained the overwhelming impression of someone who was glad that his ordeal had come to an end. Surveying him, Blizzard and Colley sensed that here was a man who had reached the end of his tether, his dishevelled appearance and unshaven features suggesting that he had not been home for several days.

'So where have you been?' asked Blizzard.

'Dossed on a friend's floor a couple of nights, spent last night on a park bench.'

'Perhaps,' said Blizzard, glancing down at the ferry ticket on the desk, 'you would like to explain why you were trying to board a boat to the Netherlands? Going on your holidays? Fancied visiting a flower festival?'

'It's not what you think.'

'Not just me thinking it, Lawrie. The cynics among us might surmise that you were trying to get away after killing Billy Guthrie.'

'Yeah, I've heard the talk,' nodded Gaines, 'but I didn't do him. Honest.'

'So if you are innocent, why flee?' asked the sergeant.

'I panicked. Roly reckoned that with Archie dying, you would think I had a good reason to kill him. Said the best thing to do was lie low for a while.'

'Such a public-spirited citizen,' murmured Blizzard. 'Where were you on Friday night?'

'That when Guthrie was killed?'

Blizzard nodded.

'I was in a boozer,' said Gaines. 'The Crown in Raglan Street. Got in there about two in the afternoon. It was a mate's birthday.'

'Can anyone vouch for that?'

'The landlord – mind, it was a lock-in so he might not welcome you asking the question. Your lot can back my story up as well.'

'Why?'

'Because my mate got rat-arsed and started a fight with another lad. Landlord kicks both of them out and it carries on in the street so your lot came and nicked them both. Don't know the name of the other bloke but my mate is called Shaun. Shaun Travis. Last time I saw, he was being driven away in a paddy wagon. One of your lot asked me for my name – I told him I was Jonny Hallam or something. I don't remember exactly; I'd had a few.'

'And why give a false name?' asked the inspector.

'Not a great time to be called Lawrie Gaines.'

'And what time was all this?' asked Blizzard.

'The kebab shop was closed, I know that, 2.30, 3.00.'

'A.M?'

'Course,' and Gaines gave a slight smile. 'I weren't nipping out for me afternoon tea.'

'I'll get someone to check it,' said Colley, leaving the room.

'So,' said Blizzard when the sergeant had gone, 'your brother died three weeks ago, I think?'

'Yeah.' The smile faded. 'He'd been bad for a couple of weeks. The medical people at the home said he'd contracted some kind of virus. We'd been there before – two or three times they prepared me for the worst but he pulled through.

You wouldn't think it to look at him but he was a tough kid, was our Archie.'

'Why was he over there, why not somewhere in Hafton?'

'The General recommended it. The doctors said it specialized in those kind of cases.'

'What kind of cases?'

'He had suffered brain damage when Guthrie attacked him. Hadn't shown at the time but it did when the swelling went down. Then when he had the stroke, it was such a shock,' and he shook his head sadly. 'A real shock. It did for my dad. I were there when he died, all he could talk about was Archie. It was like I didn't exist.'

Blizzard sought for a sense of bitterness in the comment but found nothing.

'And you were there when your brother died as well?' he asked.

'I got a call the night before,' said Gaines, tears glistening in his eyes. 'Got there for his last few hours. Roly drove me over. He's a good friend, is Roly.'

'Maybe he is – but he was also Guthrie's coach when Archie was injured. I don't understand how you can even talk to him.'

'Don't get me wrong, Mr Blizzard. For a long time I blamed Roly for what happened but in time I felt different. And I think he felt guilty that his fighter done that to Archie. I think that's why Roly used to drive me over to the home. Make up for things. But think about it – Roly Turner was a respected coach, he'd trained some really good fighters in his time. Would he really have risked throwing all that away if he had known what Guthrie was going to do? I don't think so.'

'But he did know that Eddie Gayle had money on Guthrie to win. Money changes everything.'

'Lots of punters had lots of money on lots of things that

night,' said Gaines. 'That's the nature of the game. No one did anything wrong. Well, no one apart from Guthrie.'

'Not even Eddie Gayle?'

'I ain't saying nothing about him.'

'Why do people clam up when I mention that name?' sighed Blizzard.

'I ain't scared of him.'

'Yeah, yeah.'

'Look,' said Gaines. 'Things have moved on. I have moved on. Yes, there was a time when I would have killed Guthrie but I've changed. I'm older. Got a girlfriend and a babby. Got myself responsibilities. Got the chance to do something with my life. Archie never had that chance and I ain't going to throw it away.'

'Maybe not,' said Blizzard and fixed him with a stare. 'But was there ever a time when you did try to kill Guthrie?'

The question hung in the air for a few moments and Gaines, who had retained eye contact throughout the conversation, glanced away.

'Well,' said Blizzard, 'did you try?'

'Yeah,' said Gaines quietly, 'yeah, I tried.'

It was early evening when Billy Guthrie arrived at the boxing club and sought out Roly Turner, ignoring the silent stares from all the other fighters, stares that mixed revulsion with fear. If they did not know before that you did not mix with Billy Guthrie, they sure as hell did now. The fighter's bruised and gashed face told its own story. But the boxers also knew that he had broken the code that bound them all together, that at the end of the day they were all fighters together, that nothing was worth dying for. It was one of Roly Turner's mantras when bringing on the young boxers. What Billy Guthrie had done the previous evening had changed all that. No one wanted to be seen with Billy Guthrie now.

Scanning the faces, Guthrie noticed the silent figure of Lawrie Gaines, standing over by one of the punchbags, watching him with the fire livid in his eyes. Guthrie said nothing but the merest of smiles played on his lips.

'You've got a nerve,' said Turner, emerging from the office and surveying the fighter's bruised and gashed face.

'I've got as much right as anyone to be here.'

'Like hell you do, Billy, they are going to throw the book at you and someone said the cops have been called in. I don't want no part of that. I've got my licence to think of.'

'Like I care,' shrugged Guthrie.

'What's more,' said Turner, lowering his voice, 'Eddie Gayle and his boys are still looking for you and I don't want no part of that, Billy. They've been here three times.'

'What did you tell them?'

'That I didn't know where you were but it's spooking people – I've already had a couple of fighters crying off until things settle down.'

'I'll make this quick then. Give me two grand and I'll leave the city.'

'Two grand, Billy? Like I've got that!'

'You've made plenty on my fights.' A wicked glint came into Guthrie's eye. 'And a little bird tells me that you had money on me to beat the kid. What would the boxing authorities think if they heard that the great Roly Turner had money on a fight which damn near cost another fighter his life?'

'It's all lies,' exclaimed Turner, turning to look at Gaines. 'Honest, Lawrie.'

'But who's going to prove it?' said Guthrie, with a wicked glint in his eye.

'Now hang on, Billy—'

'Give me the money and I'll be gone.'

Turner shook his head and Guthrie took a step forward, bunching his fist.

'Leave him alone,' said a voice and Lawrie Gaines walked across the gymnasium. 'You've already done enough harm.'

'Weren't my fault,' said Guthrie. 'Your brother should not have been in that ring with me. Man against boy.'

All eyes turned to Lawrie Gaines, who had started to lose his battle with emotion and now stood, fighting back the tears.

'I should kill you for that,' he said quietly.

'You and who's army, son?'

Guthrie looked round at the other boxers but to a man they averted their eyes.

'Typical,' he snorted. 'Fucking cowards. I'll give your brother one thing, he had guts.'

'And so have I, so let's settle this once and for all,' said Gaines, anger replacing grief, and nodding at the boxing ring.

'Don't talk soft.'

'Now come on, Lawrie,' said Turner, stepping between the two men. 'There is no way you are going to fight—'

'No,' said Gaines, brushing the trainer aside. 'No, Roly, I want to give this bastard the beating he deserves. Finish the job that our kid started.'

'Come on then,' said Guthrie, his voiced laced with menace as he brushed past him and walked towards the ring. 'Come on then, son. Let's see what you've got.'

'No,' said an alarmed Turner, 'I'm not letting you do this, not in my gym. I'm in enough trouble as it is.'

'If he wants to fight, I'll fight,' said Guthrie and gave a dry laugh as Gaines walked towards the ring. 'Hey, maybe you'll get a hospital bed next to your brother.'

Gaines gave an enraged roar and lunged at Guthrie. The

*older man swayed to one side and snapped out a fist,
catching his assailant on the side of the head. Gaines span
round with a startled cry and staggered backwards, his
hand going up to his busted mouth, the blood pouring from
his gashed lip. Spitting out a tooth, he lunged forwards
again but Guthrie smashed out his other fist, catching
Gaines in the face. Everyone heard the bones cracking as
the younger man clasped a hand to his nose. Without a
further word, Guthrie stalked from the room and out into
the night.*

'So you see,' said Gaines softly, 'I did try to kill him. Believe
me, if he hadn't been so strong, I would have an' all.'

He lifted a hand to his slightly bent nose. 'He left me with
a souvenir, mind.'

The door opened and Colley walked back into the room.
Blizzard glanced up at him but the sergeant shook his
head.

'Uniform confirmed his story,' said Colley, sitting down.
'Landlord backed it up as well. Reckons he didn't leave the
pub the whole time. Said he'd been on Stellas the whole
time, said he wasn't physically capable of murdering
anyone.'

'It looks,' said Blizzard wearily as he looked across the
table at Lawrie Gaines, 'like you are free to go.'

Gaines stood up.

'Just one thing before you do go,' said the inspector. 'Your
brother's fight.'

'What of it?'

'We heard that Eddie Gayle lost a lot of money because
Billy Guthrie was disqualified. Do you think there's a
chance that Gayle might have killed Guthrie because of it?'

'Who knows?' shrugged Gaines. 'I keep out of his way but
why would I care even if he did? He's done us all a favour.'

'Maybe so, but how many innocent people has he hurt down the years?' said the inspector as Gaines headed for the door. 'How many lives has he ruined?'

'Nowt to do with me.'

'Someone will have to stand up to him.'

'I told you, I ain't scared.'

'Then prove it. How many more Archies do you want there to be?'

The comment seemed to strike home and Gaines hesitated before looking back at the inspector.

'Can I trust you?' he asked.

'Depends what you have to say.'

Gaines sat back down.

'After my brother's funeral, a few of us went back to the gym for a few drinks. When everyone else had gone, me and Roly got stuck into a bottle of whisky.'

'And?'

'He told me that there had been some sort of a scam that evening.'

'Scam?' The inspector leaned forward. 'What kind of scam?'

'The word was that Gayle fixed a couple of the fights on the under-card.'

'Why?'

'Because he had an accumulator bet that night. If the fights did not all go the right way, he lost his cash. Anyway, two of the fights were shoe-ins. One was a lad called Marty Hagen against some Irish feller. It was no contest, the Paddy dropped him in the first.'

'And the other was Billy Guthrie?'

'*Should* have been Billy Guthrie. Guthrie was right, it *was* man against boy – I had even pleaded with Archie not to take the fight but he was determined, said it could be the making of him if he beat him. I mean Guthrie was still a name even though he was at the end of his career. Archie was the only one in that hall thought he could win it.'

'So where does the fixing come into it?' asked Blizzard.

'Gayle's problem was the under-card. He had four fights on the accumulator but although everyone reckoned Hagen and Guthrie were odds on, just about all the other fights were pretty even. Roly reckoned Gayle paid two of the lads to take a dive.'

'But why go to all the trouble?' asked Colley.

'Roly reckoned that Gayle had it in for a local bookie who had beaten him at a poker game. Cost him a lot of money so Gayle decided to get it back. It was all going to plan until the last bout of the fight, the one between my brother and Billy Guthrie. Gayle must have been panicking. Twenty-five grand is a lot of money in anyone's book.'

'Twenty-five grand!' exclaimed the inspector. 'Are you sure?'

'That was what Roly reckoned.'

'Then your brother threatened to ruin it all?'

'I don't think anyone realized how out of condition Guthrie was until he started to tire in the third. I don't reckon he'd trained. Typical Guthrie, always reckoned he could beat anyone.' Gaines gave a smile. 'And our kid was magnificent that night – I never knew he could fight like that. I don't think anyone did. Not even Roly. Guthrie sure as hell didn't. He said as much last week.'

'Last week?' said Blizzard slowly. 'You saw him last week? When last week?'

Gaines hesitated, the horror written large across his face.

'When?' said Blizzard, a hard edge to his voice. 'When did you see Billy Guthrie?'

'I guess you'd have found out anyway,' sighed Gaines. 'Friday.'

'Jesus Christ, Lawrie. You saw Billy Guthrie on the day he died and you didn't think to mention it?'

'Would you have done? Didn't exactly look good for me, did it? Or Roly for that matter.'

'Roly Turner was there as well?'

'Yeah, Guthrie came to see us in the gym.'

'And why,' asked the inspector, leaning forward and speaking softly, 'would he do that, Lawrie?'

'You wouldn't believe me if I told you.'

'Try me.'

'Guthrie came to say sorry.'

'Sorry? Billy Guthrie?' Blizzard raised an eyebrow.

'Yeah, I was taken aback as well. Said he wanted to apologize for what he had done to our kid.'

'Why on earth would he do that?'

'Guthrie said he was ill, something about having to spend the rest of his life on dialysis. Said he had hooked up with this woman who was going to care for him but she was a God-botherer and would only do it if he sought forgiveness for what he had done.'

'Jesus Christ,' murmured Blizzard, glancing at Colley. 'Billy Guthrie seeking forgiveness, now I've heard everything.'

'I thought exactly the same,' nodded Gaines. 'But it sounded genuine enough. Not sure I believed it, mind. Once a bastard, always a bastard.'

'Any idea if he planned to visit anyone else?'

'He reckoned he was going to see three or four people.'

'You got any names?'

'No. No, hang on, he did say he was going to see some bird. Megan something.'

'Are you sure?' said Blizzard, glancing at Colley.

'If you don't believe what I am saying, go and ask Roly Turner. He was there when all this was happening.'

'I think,' said Blizzard, 'that we will do just that.'

'Can I go now?'

'Not until I get to the bottom of this mess,' said the inspector and headed for the door before turning back and giving a slight smile. 'Don't look so downcast, Lawrie. Our custody sergeant makes the best damned bacon sandwiches this side of the Haft.'

It was shortly after 8.30 and the light was fading fast when the detectives arrived in a deserted Railway Street. Blizzard parked the car and the officers walked past the dilapidated terraces and up to the boxing club. The building was in darkness but the door was ajar.

'This does not feel right,' said Blizzard quietly.

'I agree,' nodded Colley, glancing round uneasily.

Gingerly, they pushed their way into the building, peering into the gathering gloom. Noticing a light on in the office, the officers walked across the hall, the sound of their feet reverberating round the empty gymnasium. After hesitating for a few moments, Blizzard glanced at his sergeant and pushed open the office door. Both men saw the body of Roly Turner slumped in the corner.

'I guess he'll never tell us now,' said Blizzard grimly.

'He's dead, alright,' said Colley, crouching down to peer at the body. 'I'll check that there's no one on the premises.'

'Thanks.'

'Do you reckon it was Gayle?' asked the sergeant, walking out of the office, his voice reverberating round the empty gymnasium. 'We have been rattling his cage.'

'We have indeed,' said the inspector. 'Put the word out, will you. Let's get him brought in.'

The telephone call came just as Steve McGarrity and his wife were preparing to go upstairs to bed. After standing in the hallway and listening in silence to the voice at the end,

McGarrity replaced the phone receiver and stared at his wife, who was standing in the kitchen doorway watching him with trepidation, alarmed by her husband's pale face and eyes wide with fear.

'I think,' he said quietly, 'that there's something you should know.'

chapter fourteen

The next morning, Joe Hargreaves sat staring at the telephone in his living room, hand poised over the receiver. Several times already, he had dialled the first couple of numbers then put his hand on the cancellation button. Now, finally, he dialled the full number.

'Hello, British Transport Police,' said a voice. 'Can I help you?'

'Yes,' said Hargreaves in quiet voice. 'I would like to talk to Inspector Evans.'

'So where are we with this?' asked Blizzard, walking into the squad room shortly after 9.00 and letting his gaze roam round the room. 'We really do need to tidy this one up and fast.'

'We're going as fast as we can,' said Ramsey.

'Well, work faster. The chief has already been on to Ronald three times this morning, demanding something we can put out to the press. For once, I can see his point: two unsolved murders will not exactly fill the public with confidence. Have we made any progress?'

'We've brought in as many of Turner's boxing club associates as we can,' said Ramsey and looked at Ellis. 'And I've got Fee checking his background.'

'OK,' said Blizzard, 'keep trying. And what about Eddie Gayle? This has got his ugly mitts all over it and it's the nearest we have ever got to him. Do we know where he is, Chris?'

'He's still not at home. His wife said he was away on business.'

'I'll bet he was,' grunted Blizzard. 'Keep looking. And Megan Rees? We need to find out if it's true that Guthrie came to see her. Any word?'

'Still no sign,' said Tulley. 'Neighbours reckon she said she was going away for a couple of days.'

'At least Lawrie Gaines is out of the frame,' said Colley. 'We OK to let him go, guv?'

'Yeah, fine. What I do want us to do is—' but Blizzard was interrupted by a light knock on the door.

The inspector glanced round and his face broke into a broad grin as he saw a tall uniformed officer walking into the room alongside a stooped white-haired man.

'Mick Evans, as I live and breath,' he said, walking across the room and shaking the hand of the new arrival then looking at the pensioner. 'And you must be Joe Hargreaves.'

The old man said nothing: he seemed overawed to be in the midst of so many police officers. Leaving Ramsey to marshal the murder investigation, Blizzard led the new arrivals down the corridor and into his office, where he walked over to the kettle on the windowsill.

'Cuppa?' he asked, glancing at Hargreaves.

The railman nodded. Blizzard busied himself with teabags and mugs.

'You been keeping busy then, Mick?' he asked.

'Yeah, usual stuff. A lot of cable thefts in recent weeks. They're after the copper.'

'Ah, well we might just be able to help you on that one. Remind me before you go.'

Once all three were sipping at their drinks, the inspector looked at his friend.

'So then, Mick,' he said, looking at the transport officer, 'you said that you had something that might be of interest.'

'Not sure if it is or it isn't,' said Evans. 'Joe here rang me this morning. It's my first day back. Been to Madeira; very nice.'

'All right for some,' grunted Blizzard. 'Although I can't complain, The Spur is always nice at this time of year. Something about August brings out the smell of stale urine. I hope you do not live on The Spur, Mr Hargreaves. If so, I apologize for any offence.'

'I don't live there,' said Hargreaves.

'So what's this about?' asked Blizzard, sitting back in his chair.

Evans looked at Joe Hargreaves.

'I'd rather you told it,' said the railman.

'Well,' said Evans, 'it concerns one of my old cases.'

The railway yard was virtually deserted and cast into evening shadow when Matty Hargreaves emerged from the hut, haversack slung over his shoulders, his long shift over. As he walked through the carriages on the tracks, he gave a smile as he thought of the pint he planned to have on his way home. It was the thought that had sustained him for most of what had been a sweltering summer's day. Approaching the gate on to the street, Hargreaves fumbled in his overall pocket for the keys. A sound attracted his attention and he turned to see a figure emerging through the gathering gloom. As it neared, Hargreaves felt his heart pounding faster as he realized it was Billy Guthrie.

'Billy – what you doing here?' he asked, trying not to sound frightened.

'I think you know the answer to that.'

'I ain't got no argument with you, Billy.'

'Oh, but I've got one with you, Matty.'

They were the last words Matty Hargreaves remembered until he woke up in hospital.

'Are you sure it was Guthrie who attacked him?' said Blizzard, who had listened intently to the story.

'Not until this morning. Not until Joe rang me.'

Hargreaves looked away.

'Why did it take you so long to clock that it was Guthrie, Mick?' asked Blizzard.

'Well, when we first started investigating, Matty Hargreaves would not tell us who had attacked him or why. I mean, we had our suspicions about why, of course, but we didn't know who had done it. We went back to see him several times but each time he refused even to make a complaint, so in the end, we gave up. I guess he was scared of Guthrie.'

'A familiar story. Joe,' said Blizzard, looking at the railman, who had listened to the story in silence, occasionally dabbing at moist eyes with a handkerchief, 'would your brother speak to us now that Guthrie has gone?'

Joe shook his head.

'Slight problem there,' said Evans. 'A year after the attack, Matty dropped dead. He'd been suffering seizures for several months. The doctors said it was one of those that did for him.'

Hargreaves dabbed at his eyes with his handkerchief.

'Were the seizures connected to the attack?'

'The doctors could not say for sure, but you've got to assume so. He'd never had them before and the scan he had after the attack did show up some scarring of the brain.'

'He went through Hell,' said Hargreaves quietly. 'Fit after fit, it were awful to behold. No man deserves that. I owe it to Matty to put this right. Roly suggested I do it.'

'Roly Turner?' said Blizzard quickly.

'Aye. He came to see me. I didn't want to ring Mr Evans at first, couldn't see no point to it, but then when I heard on the radio that Roly were dead—' His voice tailed off.

'So what did you tell Inspector Evans?'

'It was just before my brother died,' said Hargreaves quietly. 'He knew he were dying. Nobody had told him but he knew. He were in hospital and suddenly he grasps my hand and tells me that it were Guthrie did it to him.'

'Why did he not tell anyone earlier?'

'He were frightened. Guthrie was a wicked man.' Hargreaves showed the first signs of anger since he had walked into the room. 'A truly wicked man. Matty said he were afeared that Guthrie would come back for his wife or one of the bairns if word got out that he had been talking to the police. Told me to keep it secret.'

'And you did?'

'Aye.'

'So what happened to change things?'

'Guthrie turned up at the house on Friday morning.'

'Your house?' said Blizzard.

'Aye, I couldn't believe it. Said he were sorry for what happened to Matty.'

'And you accepted his apology?'

'I just wanted him to leave, didn't believe he were really sorry,' and the anger was back in Hargreaves's voice again. 'I tell you, Mr Blizzard, if I had been twenty years younger, I'd have lamped the bastard. Sitting there drinking my tea and saying he were sorry like that made everything all right. I don't reckon Roly believed it either.'

'So where does Roly fit into it?'

'We worked together on the railways. Hadn't seen him for years but somehow he knew what Guthrie had done and that he had come to see me. With Guthrie dead, Roly said it were time to tell the police about what he did to our Matty.'

169

'Do you know why Guthrie attacked your brother?' asked Blizzard.

'Mr Evans always reckoned it were to do with all the trouble.'

Blizzard looked at Evans.

'Trouble?'

Evans was about to reply when Colley stuck his head round the office door.

'Sorry to interrupt, guv,' he said, 'but uniform have just lifted Eddie Gayle. And his lawyer is threatening to sue you.'

'No originality,' sighed Blizzard. 'Lawyers have no originality.'

'I'm sorry, love,' said the man at the pound. 'Really I am.'

Megan Rees stared down in silence at the dead body of her dog.

'Some sort of virus or something,' continued the man. 'We got the vet in but there weren't nothing we could do about it. Came on real quick.'

Megan Rees turned and walked out of the building. Once in the street, she pulled out of her pocket a crumpled newspaper cutting and stared down at the picture of Fee Ellis.

Eddie Gayle sat in the interview room and calmly eyed Blizzard and his sergeant. He did not seem unsettled by the predicament in which he found himself. His confidence was well founded because every time he walked free from such encounters, his sense of invincibility grew, the mocking smile became wider and his bravado more pronounced. Over the years, he had become increasingly adept at playing the game, his lawyer often lodging official complaints against the police, John Blizzard in particular. His campaign had made many officers reluctant to move against him and John Blizzard hated him for it. And with every passing day, his hatred for Eddie Gayle became deeper. Indeed, there had been times over the years when he had been forced to ask himself if it was becoming an obsession. Not that he cared if it was: all Blizzard wanted was to see him behind bars.

Arthur Ronald knew all this and when Blizzard rang him at home the night before to say he wanted to bring Gayle in for questioning, the superintendent had sighed, knowing the problems it would inevitably cause. Indeed, so delicate had the situation become the year before that the superintendent had even been summoned to see the chief constable after yet another complaint of harassment from Gayle. The result was that Ronald was forced to instruct his officers, Blizzard among them, to go easy on Gayle. Such a ruling did not sit well with the superintendent but the chief constable had brushed aside his protests, yet another incident in the deteriorating relationship between the two men. For his part, Blizzard hated the chief constable for the ruling almost as much as he hated Gayle.

However, on receiving Blizzard's call, Ronald had immediately seen the sense of the inspector's request and given his approval without even checking with the chief constable. So it was that Blizzard now sat in the interview room at Abbey Road and eyed Gayle with thinly disguised distaste. Perspiring as ever, with stains forming on the armpits of his dark suit, Gayle mopped his brow in the oppressive heat of the small room. Sitting next to Gayle was Paul D'Arcy, no stranger to police attention. A local lawyer who had become immensely, and mysteriously, rich, he was a thin-faced man in his late thirties, dressed immaculately in a dark pinstripe suit with a white handkerchief poking out its breast pocket. A man who had helped Eddie Gayle wheedle his way out of more than a few tight spots over the years, D'Arcy interested the police greatly. Alerted to the lawyer's wealth by his large house on the western side of the city, and the expensive cars parked on its gravelled drive, detectives had long suspected him of laundering dirty money for organized crime in the city.

'Right from the outset, I wish to place on the record that this is harassment of my client,' said D'Arcy tartly.

Blizzard smiled thinly. It was always the same opening gambit with Paul D'Arcy. Same old, same old.

'And,' continued the lawyer, 'I want to make it abundantly clear that we regard my client's arrest as part of a relentless campaign by the police, particularly you, Blizzard, to blacken Mr Gayle's good name.'

'Pha! What good name?'

'What's this about, anyway?' asked Gayle. 'I parked my Jag on a double yellow line again?'

'We are investigating the murder of Roly Turner.'

'Yeah, I heard about that on the radio. Pity. Nice man.' Gayle made no attempt to make the words seem sincere. 'But I know nothing about that.'

'Word is that you were at the gym on Sunday night.'

'My client,' said D'Arcy quickly, 'is a benefactor of many local community organizations. He believes that, having come from humble beginnings, it is important that he puts some of his wealth back into the community.'

'The only reason he would want to support a boxing club is to pick up some muscle,' said Blizzard dismissively.

'A comment which does not warrant reply, Chief Inspector. However, I am sure that if we looked back through our records, we would discover that my client made a charitable donation to the gymnasium some time in the past. It may have been that the weekend's visit was him checking up on the benefits derived from his investment.'

'But he can't remember?'

'He makes so many donations.'

'Oh, for God's sake,' exclaimed Blizzard.

'What particularly interests us,' said Colley, seeking to calm the atmosphere, 'is your client's links with events twelve years ago.'

'Events?' asked D'Arcy, glancing at his client. 'What events?'

'A fight in which a young man called Archie Gaines was severely injured.' Colley looked at Gayle. 'Does the name sound familiar to you?'

'Never heard of him. Archie, you say?'

'Come on, Eddie,' said Blizzard irritably, 'you know exactly who we are talking about.'

'I meet so many people.'

'Then let me refresh your memory – he was the kid knocked out by Billy Guthrie.'

'Guthrie? Nope, sorry, that name does not ring a bell – as it were.'

'Bloody Hell,' exclaimed Blizzard. 'This is not a sodding game!'

'Ah,' said Gayle, a smile playing on his lips, 'but it is.'

Blizzard sighed. It was always like this when they had Gayle in for questioning. However, despite his growing annoyance, he remained in control of his emotions and satisfied himself with glaring over the table at his adversary.

'Twelve years ago,' he said, leaning forward, 'you fixed a couple of fights.'

'Prove it.'

'Well, it certainly becomes more difficult now that the man with all the answers is dead.'

Gayle said nothing.

'You may be silent, Eddie,' said Colley, 'but there's others are talking.'

'What people?' asked Gayle: he looked worried for the first time.

'Never mind what people but suffice to say the death of Roly has touched a few consciences. There's plenty of people would love to see us arrest someone for his murder. I am sure they would be delighted if that person was you.'

'I do hope that you are not threatening my client,' said D'Arcy coldly.

'All I am saying is that there are people happy to testify that your charitable client fixed those fights twelve years ago as part of his attempts to ensure a £25,000 pay-off. Not desperately charitable, Eddie.'

'Is that what this is about?' said Gayle, sounding relieved at the angle the questioning was taking. 'What if I did fix a couple of fights? Don't mean nothing and it certainly don't mean I killed Turner. You are fishing, as usual.'

'But it is a remarkable coincidence,' said Blizzard. 'I mean, not only is Roly Turner dead but so is the man who cost you the twenty-five grand in the first place.'

'So?'

'We are wondering if it might just be possible that when Guthrie came back to the city, you decided to settle some old scores. Perhaps you were worried that he would start talking to us. We understand that Guthrie came back to make amends for some of his previous actions. Say sorry.'

'Guthrie say sorry!' exclaimed Gayle. 'That'll be the day.'

'Thought you didn't know him,' said Blizzard.

Gayle glowered at him.

'Look, Eddie,' continued the inspector. 'I am perfectly prepared to be generous and believe that your boys went too far, that you did not mean for Guthrie to be killed. Maybe it was the same with Roly. The pathologist says he died of a heart attack. Maybe all you wanted was him roughing up a bit and it went wrong.'

'Now why would I do that?' said Gayle innocently.

'Because it's what you do.'

'This is all nothing but supposition,' said D'Arcy dismissively. He stood up and clipped closed his briefcase. 'Wild guesswork as usual and unless you have any firm evidence, myself and my client are leaving. And my guess is that you don't.'

Blizzard did not reply.

'Besides,' said Gayle, also standing up. 'Why would I want to kill someone over twenty-five grand? It's nothing to me, Blizzard, do you hear? Nothing.'

'It sounds a lot to me, Eddie,' said Blizzard.

'Maybe it does to a plod,' leered Gayle and held out his arm to reveal a watch, 'but this cost more than that.'

And with that, Eddie Gayle walked out into the corridor. His mocking laughter hung in the air long after he had gone.

It was early evening when Megan Rees stood among the lengthening shadows in the street outside Abbey Road Police Station and stared silently at the building. She glanced down at the newspaper cutting in her hand, reading the article telling the story of Fee Ellis being commended for disarming a man with a knife. Ellis, the article said, had been described as 'extremely courageous' by the chief constable. Megan Rees carefully folded the newspaper cutting and returned it to her coat pocket.

chapter fifteen

Dusk was falling as Blizzard sat in his office, deep in contemplation, ignoring the rapidly cooling mug of tea clasped in his hand. He glanced at the pile of reports on his desk and sighed: the team had been working hard to link Eddie Gayle with the murder of Roly Turner, to link anyone with it, but had failed so far. Blizzard picked up the top document. It was from Graham Ross: the inspector could hear the DI's apologetic tone in every word as the report indicated that there was nothing definite to point to the killer of the boxing trainer. Blizzard flicked through the other reports. Blank, blank, blank. And yet, he sensed that they were tantalizingly close to breaking the case wide open: it just needed that final piece of the jigsaw. He closed his eyes and tried to clear his mind. There was a light knock on the door.

'You still here?' asked Blizzard as Colley walked in.

'No, I'm a hologram, the real David Colley has got a life.'

Blizzard gave a weary smile.

'Actually, I'm just off now,' said the sergeant, dragging up a chair and sitting down. 'Not sure there's much we can do now.'

'Ramsey reckons we are not getting much further on Roly Turner?'

'Not really.'

'Hargreaves?'

'Waiting for some calls back but it's certainly interesting. The whole thing has been a beggar, though – so many people had reason to see Billy Guthrie dead.'

'OK,' said Blizzard and wafted a hand at the door. 'Go on, go home. What is it tonight?'

'Hill Street Blues,' said Colley, getting up and heading for the door. 'Good night, guv.'

'Good night, David,' said Blizzard.

He was about to head for home himself when the phone on his desk rang.

'Blizzard,' he said, picking up the receiver.

'Hello, stranger,' said a woman's voice.

'Wendy Talbot, how the devil are you?' said the inspector delightedly.

Blizzard had worked with the Regional Crime Squad detective chief inspector on a previous case and, sitting in his office now, visualized the deceptively slight woman with her short brown hair starting to grey at the temples and narrow, angular features. Blizzard knew that when it came to solving crime, there were few better. A call from Wendy Talbot offered much promise.

'Still at the office then,' said Talbot.

'As are you, by the sound of it. What can I do you for?'

'It seems that you and I might just have a joint interest. Saw the picture you circulated of William Guthrie. You wanted to know where he has been for the past few years.'

'Certainly do,' said Blizzard, leaning forward and reaching for a pen and notepad. 'You got something?'

'We believe that he has been living in Sheffield under the name Leonard Riley. He's a bit of a mess in your picture but I've checked it with several of the team and we're happy to say it's him.'

'A lot of people have been happy to say it's him.'

'Yeah, sounds like he's got a pretty murky past. Anyway, to make sure, we did some discreet checking.'

'RCS? Discreet? You mean you didn't smash your way through their front door?'

'I don't know,' said Talbot. 'You try to help someone.'

Her voice did not suggest that she was offended by the comment. Such banter was the way of things when you dealt with John Blizzard: he had never made any secret of the fact that he regarded RCS as what he termed 'glory boys'. It was the reason he had turned down an approach to join their ranks some years before.

'Anyway, as I was saying,' continued Talbot, 'we made some discreet inquiries and no one has seen Lenny Riley since Thursday afternoon. Although I have to admit that our officer could not hear very well because he was dangling out of a helicopter and strafing the street with machine gun fire at the time.'

Blizzard roared with laughter.

'Touché, Wendy,' he said. 'Touché. Anyway, why is Regional Crime Squad interested in Billy Guthrie in the first place?'

'To be honest, we're not. We're more interested in his business partner. Actually, your guy Guthrie is a bit of a mystery. No one seems to know much about him before he arrived in Sheffield.'

'Which would fit with him changing his identify when he left Hafton.'

'I guess so. Anyway, what we do know is that a few years ago, he hooked up with a local businessman who owns a scrapyard in Sheffield.'

'Bent, presumably?'

'But of course. He's got previous for handling stolen goods, including thefts from railway yards. For the copper, cables, pipework, oh, and lead from churches.'

'One of Guthrie's little peccadilloes when he was in Hafton.'

'So I gather but, like I say, our attention has been mainly focused on his business partner. He's the front man, the one swanning around in the flash car and wearing the flash jewellery. We think he's the one running the gang, although I guess your guy must know what's happening.'

'I am sure he does. Why are you so interested, though? It's only a bit of knock-off gear, surely? I know we mere mortals struggle with big crime but I am sure Sheffield CID could handle it.'

'The more we looked at it, the bigger it became. It seems that the scrapyard is at the centre of a major network with stuff brought in from all over the north. Not sure where your mate Guthrie fits into it.'

'Have you found anything out about Guthrie's family, by any chance? We're trying to find out who might have had a motive to murder him. We wondered about the wife and kid. Any sign of them during your inquiries?'

'Seems she left him five or six years ago and took the kid with her. There was rumour that they went into a refuge because Guthrie was beating up the wife. No idea where they are now. Not that we have looked particularly hard, mind. Maybe they changed their name to get away from him.'

'Can't blame them for that,' said Blizzard.

'Mind, another reason we have not been particularly interested in Guthrie is that he seems to have become a changed man over the past two or three years. Lives with a local woman, a real stalwart from the local church. Guthrie even helps out with Sunday services. Damn it, Blizzard, I must be coming over all forgiving in my old age. Sorry.'

'We heard that he was a bit of a reformed character as well. Maybe it's true.'

'And maybe it's not.'

'Before I forget, what was the name of Guthrie's business partner? The one you fancy?'

'Roberts. Barry Roberts.'

'In which case,' beamed Blizzard, 'I might just be able to help you there, Wendy. In fact, we might just be able to help each other out. We would love an excuse to make some – how can we phrase it? – indiscreet inquiries.'

Half an hour later, there was a knock on the office door and in walked Arthur Ronald, for once not wearing a suit but dressed instead in a pale-blue shirt and black trousers.

'This had better be good,' he said, lowering himself heavily into the chair. 'I was just about to take a bath.'

'Too much information already,' said the inspector.

'So what you got?'

'Our calling card for The Spur. Just had Wendy Talbot on the phone. They reckon they can link The Spur to a major thieving ring. They are wondering if some of The Spur's bad lads might not be involved somewhere – stealing stuff to order. The guy at the centre of it all just happens to be Barry Roberts, the uncle of our friend Terry.'

'Not the kid who took a header off the railway museum?'

'The very same. And that means—'

'That we can go in mob-handed,' beamed Ronald, then his face clouded over. 'Hang on, are the RCS happy with all of this? They normally carry on alarmingly if we try to piss on their bonfire.'

'They were just about ready to move anyway. When they found out Guthrie had been murdered, they decided to bring everything forward before it spooks the rest. Wendy is quite happy for us to do our stuff at this end while they do Sheffield. It's got to be better than trying to convince the chief that we're after Barnie.'

Ronald looked bemused.

'Barnie?'

'The purple dinosaur,' explained Blizzard, tapping the side of his nose conspiratorially. 'You really do need to keep up to date with the villains working our patch.'

'Sometimes,' said Ronald, standing up to go, 'I wonder if you shouldn't take more holiday. Oh, while I'm in, I hear that you've released Eddie Gayle?'

'I wasn't going to tell you until tomorrow. How come you know?'

'Because I was just about to get into the bath—'

'Will you stop saying that? It really is not the kind of image that you want kicking about your mind when you're trying to sleep at night.'

Ronald gave him a hard look.

'So how *do* you know about Gayle?' asked Blizzard.

'Because his solicitor has been on to HQ, demanding to talk to the chief. They rang me instead. I take it we can't charge him with anything?'

'Sorry, Arthur,' shrugged Blizzard. 'Usual story, nothing to tie him to anything. Like he says, so he fixed a couple of boxing matches, so what? It happened twelve years ago; who would care?'

'Someone cared enough to kill Roly Turner.'

'They did,' nodded Blizzard, 'but I just can't see Eddie Gayle doing it. He as good as admitted he fixed the fights. In fact, he was damned near boasting about it. If he did kill Roly to keep him quiet, why admit that? It doesn't make sense. Besides, Eddie doesn't make mistakes.'

'So we're no further forward?' said Ronald, heading for the door.

'Actually,' said Blizzard enigmatically, 'we might just be. See there's this old fellow called Joe Hargreaves. Don't say much but when he does speak—'

chapter sixteen

The last embers of evening sunshine were fading through the belt of trees ringing the police station when John Blizzard arrived at Abbey Road the following night and walked slowly through deserted corridors to his office. He had deliberately arrived early to compose his thoughts before everyone else started to gather. Once in his office, with the room illuminated by the little table lamp, he sat in the shadows and considered the events which were about to unfold.

The call from Wendy Talbot the previous evening had been a welcome one. So engrossed had the inspector become in the murders of Billy Guthrie and Roly Turner that his attention had wandered from The Spur. Now, John Blizzard was grimly satisfied that his attention had turned once more to the estate. Not normally a man who felt the pressure of expectation, this time was different for John Blizzard as he sat in his office. The inspector knew that, despite the involvement of the Regional Crime Squad, Arthur Ronald had still been forced to put his neck on the line to persuade the reluctant chief constable to sanction the raid on The Spur. And persuade was the word: the superintendent had left for headquarters shortly after ten that morning but the call had not come until early afternoon, the inspector becoming increasingly edgy when it failed to materialize. When it did arrive, Blizzard was in his office.

'It's Arthur,' said the superintendent. 'The man from del Monte, he say yes.'

'So the RCS do come in useful for something,' Blizzard had said, feeling a rush of relief.

'It's only partly that, John,' Ronald had said gravely. 'Before I could open my mouth, I got the real fifth degree over having two unsolved murders on the patch. The chief is unhappy at the way the papers are reporting it. I suggested that raiding The Spur would be good PR.'

'And he went for that? Surely, it's all the bad PR that spooked him in the first place?'

'That's why we can't afford to fuck it up – his words not mine,' Ronald had said.

Sitting in his office now, Blizzard knew why he felt so uneasy as the superintendent's words reverberated round his head: the cost of the operation going wrong would be high for both men. If Blizzard's relationship with the chief constable was poor, then Ronald's was little better. It had started to deteriorate the moment Ronald was chosen as the man to head up CID in the force's southern half and immediately announced that he wanted John Blizzard to lead the Western Division team, an utterance that appalled the chief constable. Ever the astute politician, Ronald knew exactly what he was doing in making such a request, realizing that there were many in headquarters, primarily uniformed officers, all strategies and policy documents, who detested his friend's plain-spoken ways and would not want to see him elevated to a position of greater influence.

Faced with the embarrassment of his new superintendent declining the promotion when everyone knew the job had already been offered, the chief constable had reluctantly backed down. There were those who believed that Ronald's card was marked from that day but his ensuing success in bringing crime down and pushing detection rates up, helped by the performance of a revitalized Western Division CID under John Blizzard, had long since vindicated the superintendent's judgement. For his part, Blizzard had always deeply appreciated his friend's unstinting support. Now, walking over to the window and staring out into the gathering darkness, the chief inspector felt the enormity of the moment. He knew the feeling was about more than the personal risks that both men were taking with their careers: they had taken them before and survived. No, he knew that real reason he felt anxious was the memory of that night when Kenny Jarvis died, an evening never far from the inspector's thoughts. John Blizzard had dealt with many murders in his career, seen many bodies, arrested many villains, but there was something about the death of a fellow officer that made it feel different, a sense that one of the family had been taken from them. Even though Blizzard had hardly known the lad – it had taken him six months after the constable transferred to Abbey Road to discover his Christian name – he had nevertheless felt close to him as he began the investigation into his murder. Had felt close to him many times since, felt close to him now as the inspector stood silently in his office. Suddenly, he was assailed by the strong sensation that Jarvis was standing behind him. Feeling the hairs standing up on the back of his neck, the inspector resisted the temptation to turn round for the best part of a minute. Eventually, he gave in and turned but there was no one there.

'Must be cracking up,' he murmured.

But he knew that Kenny Jarvis had been there, if only in spirit. His presence was one that had not left Abbey Road since the night he died. Perhaps tonight, thought Blizzard, perhaps tonight it could be banished. And, for all the stark differences between his way of policing and that of his chief constable, John Blizzard nevertheless found himself understanding the one thing that bound them together: the fear that it could happen again, that there could be another Kenny Jarvis on their watch. That it would be their responsibility. Staring into the night now, the darkness thickening by the second, the chief inspector recalled again the sense of shock that had pervaded the police station for months after the murder of Kenny Jarvis, a shock replaced by anger as days turned to weeks. He recalled the growing tension in the days leading up to the crown court case: when the jury returned their verdicts of guilty on all three men, it had brought about a sense of relief that the inspector had rarely experienced.

He smiled slightly as he recalled the drunken night that followed with just about every officer in Western Division heading for their local pub, a cavernous hostelry standing on the corner of Abbey Road. Much ale had been consumed – the latter stages of the celebrations were a little bit of a haze for Blizzard although there had been suggestions that he had danced at some stage – and rarely had he felt so appreciated as uniformed officer after uniformed officer congratulated him on leading the successful investigation. However, what Blizzard remembered most was the way the room fell silent as the dead constable's parents had arrived unexpectedly and his mother had issued a halting and heartfelt thanks for the efforts of all the officers who had brought her son's killers to justice. Blizzard remembered now how Kenny's mother had walked up to him, supported on her husband's arm, and had reached up and gently kissed him. Blizzard's hand went instinctively up to his right cheek now.

He glanced up at the clock and sighed. Still an hour to go and the minute hand appeared not to have moved since last he looked at it. In an effort to make himself busy, he sat

185

down behind the desk and reached for the top document in his in-tray. It was from the HR department and he sighed. There was a knock on the door and Colley walked in. Something about the sergeant's demeanour alerted the chief inspector that something was wrong. Badly wrong.

'Got those names you wanted from Mick Evans,' said Colley quietly, handing over a piece of paper. 'The ones in the frame for Matty Hargreaves. I'm sorry.'

Blizzard scanned them and looked up sharply at the sergeant.

'We sure about this?'

'We double-checked them with him. Not saying they are right but we have to ask the question.'

Blizzard stared down at the sheet of paper again and did not even notice when the sergeant left the room. The chief inspector was still staring at it when Ronald entered the office ten minutes later.

'Ah,' said the superintendent, lowering himself into a chair and noticing that the inspector was still holding the document, 'doing the paperwork. How commendable.'

'Just keeping myself busy,' said Blizzard, screwing the sheet up and shying it at the wastepaper bin.

'And there was me rather hoping that all my lectures on the importance of administration in the modern police service had finally achieved the desired effect,' said Ronald wistfully. 'One can but dream.'

Ronald noticed the inspector's distracted air. 'You OK?'

'Yeah, I'm fine. Just … well, you know.'

'I know. You ready?'

'As ready as I ever will be,' said Blizzard. 'I've had Ramsey draw up a list of target addresses.'

'Well, make sure he's got the right ones.'

'He has. Oh, and Colley has come up with some interesting stuff as well.'

'Did I hear that you sent him home earlier?'

'He's back now but, yeah, I gave him a couple of hours off – told him to make sure he did the baby's bathtime.'

'The softer side of John Blizzard,' said Ronald with a disbelieving shake of the head. 'Who would have thought it?'

'Yeah, but make sure it does not get out.'

'Your secret is safe with me, sunshine,' said Ronald with a smile. 'Good to hear that you are looking after David, though.'

'Told him to take a week's leave when this little lot is done and dusted. The lad's out on his feet.'

'You'll be the same when you have a little 'un.'

'Don't,' shuddered Blizzard. 'I get enough of it at home.'

'Why be like that? Kids are a joy, an absolute joy – apart, obviously, from the cost. Do you know, I read a newspaper article the other day that said that having a kid costs £184,000 once you have taken into account university and food and their accommodation and all the other expenses, running them round all the time, all those kind of things. Actually, what we did was set up a special building society account at a fixed interest rate then transferred some of the money to … what?'

'You make fatherhood sound such a delight,' grinned Blizzard.

'Well, it is,' said Ronald and gave his friend a rueful look. 'Just a bloody expensive one, that's all.'

'It's the cost that worries me, I guess.'

Ronald looked at his friend intently.

'I was just thinking of the night after the court case,' explained Blizzard. 'You know, when Kenny's folks came to the do? Seeing them so broken up about what had happened, it made me think. Kids, you know. I went to see mum a few weeks ago; she'll never be the same. There's pictures of him everywhere in the house.'

'It's the price of loving, John.'

'I know, but it's like he's not dead.'

'Maybe he's not.'

'What makes you say that?' asked the inspector sharply.

'Don't you feel him here sometimes?'

Blizzard nodded and the men sat in silence for a few moments then Blizzard glanced at the clock.

'Are we right about this, Arthur?' he asked. 'I mean, if it goes wrong tonight, and the police end up looking stupid, we're finished. The chief will see to that.'

'I didn't think you did doubts.'

'Yes, but ... well, you know,' Blizzard's voice tailed off. 'Thinking of Kenny and all that. And what happened on Saturday night. We could easily have lost someone. The lads were very lucky. We won't always be.'

'Yeah, I know,' and Ronald shrugged, 'but if it goes wrong, it goes wrong. It comes with the territory.'

'I know but—'

'Listen, you and I have talked about this enough times. The point is that we are seen to be there. On that estate. Tonight. In force. What was it you said the day you became DCI? There are no no-go zones, you said. I clearly recall you scrawling it across the noticeboard in the CID room in big red letters.'

'It's still there.'

'Except someone rewrote it with neater writing.'

'Ramsey did that,' said Blizzard. 'My untidy scrawl offended his sense of order in the universe.'

'And he does all his paperwork,' said Ronald pointedly, glancing at the wastepaper bin.

There was a knock on the door and the uniformed superintendent walked in. A tall man in his early fifties, with thinning ginger hair and the slightest of moustaches, Jerry Hart nodded at Blizzard and drew up a chair. Blizzard

eyed him in surprise: he could not recall Hart ever being in
his office, not least because the inspector's relationship with
uniform had tended to be fractious down the years. He had
offended too many senior officers with his outspoken
comments for it to be any different. Indeed, he had fallen out
with Hart on several occasions.

'Ready?' asked Ronald, glancing at his counterpart.

'All set,' nodded Hart. 'I've brought in some extra bodies.'

'Extra? I thought we already had plenty.'

'A bit of insurance,' said the superintendent, tapping the
side of his nose enigmatically. 'You never know.'

'How much insurance?' asked Ronald.

'Come with me,' said Hart.

The three of them walked down the corridors in silence,
the uniformed superintendent with an enigmatic smile on
his face. Eventually, the sound of voices growing louder, they
pushed their way through a large set of doors and emerged
into the yard at the back of the station. Blizzard's jaw
dropped as he surveyed the scene: ranged before him were
more than twenty police vans, a dozen squad cars and a
special incident truck. Milling in between them were more
than a hundred uniformed officers, checking their
equipment and talking in excited voices about the operation
to come. Glancing over to one corner of the yard, the
inspector saw Brian Robertshaw, his face still bruised from
the attack at the weekend. The sergeant caught his eye and
nodded. Blizzard returned the gesture.

'Jesus,' breathed the inspector, turning to look at Hart.
'Where did you get all them from?'

'The moment word got out that we were going into The
Spur, every police officer this side of the water wanted to be
involved. East have sent a couple of vanloads over as well
and there's at least one team from Burniston. There's a few
I've never seen before. For all I know, they're just members

of the public who fancied being involved. Oh, and I've got three ARVs. Just in case.'

'Insurance indeed,' murmured Blizzard.

'We nearly lost two good officers on that estate,' said the superintendent with a sudden fierceness. 'It's payback time.'

'And in answer to your earlier question, John,' said Ronald. 'Yes, we are right.'

chapter seventeen

Blizzard had never seen the briefing room at Abbey Road so full and the sight gladdened his heart: he loved an audience. The sense of anticipation at Abbey Road had been growing steadily for the previous half an hour as more and more officers filtered in from the yard to take their places. Now, the clock was approaching midnight and the assembled officers sat and watched the chief inspector as he made his way through their ranks to the front, the detective occasionally pausing to shake a hand or nod at an old acquaintance.

On reaching the front, the inspector let his gaze roam round the room, settling briefly on every person in turn, a trick he had used for years and one designed to make every officer feel that they were an integral part of the operation to come. The inspector's gaze settled briefly on Colley, leaning in his customary position against the wall at the back of the room. Next to him stood Chris Ramsey, the detective inspector constantly fidgeting as he tried to control the nerves that always consumed him on such occasions. Blizzard was not worried: he knew that once the action had started, Chris Ramsey was as dependable as they came.

Letting his gaze run through the ranks of uniformed officers, Blizzard spotted some of his other CID officers as well, Fee sitting next to a burly firearms officer, Tulley at the end of a row and in the process of consuming a chocolate bar, several younger constables in the front. The inspector was assailed, and surprised, by an overwhelming sense of family. He glanced to his right where Arthur Ronald sat, who gave the DCI a nod.

'Ladies and gentlemen,' began Blizzard, his voice quiet to begin with, 'thank you for turning up at this hour. I know that many of you are off duty and that some have come in off leave: your presence is greatly appreciated. See, I can be nice to uniform.'

He paused to let the laughter ripple round the room.

'But,' he said, a sudden steel in his voice. 'I do not need to tell you that we are going in tonight because we damn near lost two colleagues on The Spur on Saturday. Garry Canham is still in hospital but Brian is here tonight and we are delighted to see him.'

Applause ran round the room. Robertshaw nodded his appreciation and seemed close to tears.

'So let me remind you why we are going in tonight,' said Blizzard when the applause had died away. 'For too long, the villains on The Spur have been allowed to get away with their crimes virtually unchecked. I am sure we have all seen the memo. Well, tonight that changes. The Spur seems to be part of a network operating across the north and they'll thieve just about anything. As we sit here, Regional Crime Squad officers are about to launch a series of raids in Sheffield.'

A murmur ran round the room.

'Your team leaders have details of the properties which we will raid,' continued Blizzard. 'Oh, and make sure you read the bloody dockets right – I don't want anyone barging in on some old wrinkly on the toilet. It'd give the poor old girl a heart attack.'

Blizzard gave a thin smile and there were some half-laughs.

'Anyway,' he continued, 'suffice for me to say that this is a show of force, a clear message to the criminals on The Spur that we will no longer tolerate their behaviour. Tonight, ladies and gentlemen, we take The Spur back.'

Applause rang round the room.

'And I do not want us to waste this opportunity,' said the inspector, 'so I want anything. We're not just after the gang. I want to see us seize drugs, weapons, anything. If their tax disc is out of date, I want them nicked.'

'What tax disc?' said a voice.

'I assume,' said Blizzard, 'that was one of our esteemed colleagues from traffic? And yes, you can check the tread on the tyres if you want. Anything over eight millimetres and we'll throw the book at the bastards.'

More laughter.

'So,' said Blizzard, 'whatever we do, let's make tonight worthwhile. If we balls things up, it will be a long time before we are back on that estate. By the end of tonight, I want that stupid memo to have been torn up.'

Many of the officers nodded their heads.

'There is one more thing,' said Blizzard, holding up a hand: the soft tone of his voice brought a hush to the gathering. He glanced over at Arthur Ronald. 'I know that tonight is not about Kenny Jarvis but I know that many of you will feel him riding with you when you go on to that estate. And I know that you are angry about what happened to the boys on Saturday. However, let's keep it professional and keep your wits about you. Please remember that The Spur is a dangerous place to be. We saw on Saturday what they are capable of doing.'

The inspector paused to let his words have their effect.

'So,' he said, looking across the room to where Colley was standing, 'let's do it to them before they do it to us.'

The sergeant grinned, there was a scraping of chairs and a ripple of excited murmuring as the officers headed for the door. Ronald walked over to the inspector and placed a hand gently on his shoulder.

'Good stuff,' he said.

'Did you like the end bit?' said Blizzard cheerfully. 'I got it from Hill Street Blues.'

Tommy Rafferty stood at the window of his flat on The Spur and looked out over the darkened quadrangle.

'It's only a matter of time,' he said, turning into the room and looking at Steve McGarrity, who was sitting at the table nursing a can of beer and reading the sports pages of the local newspaper.

'Don't worry about it,' said McGarrity, not even glancing up from the paper. 'Blizzard will be too busy chasing after Eddie Gayle to worry about anything else.'

'Yeah, but—'

'You know what he's like. If Blizzard thinks that Gayle is involved he'll do everything he can to prove it. There's no way he's going to bother about this place.'

'He's bound to come soon, though,' said Rafferty nervously, returning his gaze to the deserted quadrangle.

'Relax, Tommy, for God's sake.'

'It's not that easy.'

'What do you see, Tommy?' said McGarrity, finally looking up from the racing results and coming to join him at the window.

'Eh?'

'What do you see?'

Rafferty peered through the curtains again.

'Nothing.'

'Exactly.' McGarrity downed the remainder of his beer and walked over to the fridge to get another can. 'You got anything else apart from Tennents?'

'Sorry, Steve, that's all I've got. What has me not seeing owt in the quadrangle got to do with it?'

'Think about it,' said McGarrity, returning to the table and cracking open the can. 'What has happened at the weekend? Your delightful neighbours damn near killed a couple of cops and Terry Roberts takes a header off the museum roof. And what do the police do? Nothing. Nothing at all. There hasn't been a police officer within half a mile of this place for the past two days, from what I hear.'

'Yes but—'

'When did you last see a plod on the estate?'

'Blizzard on Sunday.'

'And how long was he here?'

'I don't know, twenty minutes.'

'Exactly,' said McGarrity. 'Twenty minutes. Anywhere else and they would be swarming all over the place.'

'That's what worries me.'

'I tell you, Tommy, the chief constable has told them to lay off the estate. And if even if they did come, they wouldn't come for us. Blizzard would keep us out of it. Take my word for it.'

'I'm not sure. Blizzard always says that—'

'Blizzard,' snorted McGarrity, returning his attention to the sports pages. 'This is way above his head. I tell you, Tommy, the cops are running scared. You can stop worrying about them. They're not going to do anything.'

chapter eighteen

The convoy of police vehicles rolled into the main quadrangle of The Spur shortly before 12.30, their wheels crunching on the broken glass. Blizzard was travelling in the front of the leading van and, as the vehicle slowed to a halt in the centre of the square, the inspector jumped out and looked quickly around him. Noticing curtains flickering in several of the windows on the upper landings and one or two figures already moving in the shadows, the inspector scowled. He hated The Spur and he hated the vast majority of its occupants but, most of all, he hated the way it had been allowed to get into this state. Perhaps, he told himself, something would change after tonight's operation. He doubted it.

Standing by the van, he watched with grim satisfaction as officers poured from the vehicles and started fanning out across the square, their equipment clinking in the silence. Behind him, uniformed officers carrying riot shields moved rapidly to form a cordon so that no one could escape from the quadrangle through the tunnel. The teams had been told that speed was crucial, that they needed to secure the estate before the residents could mount any kind of defence, that there was to be no repeat of Saturday's events. Blizzard knew that similar scenes were being enacted in the other squares. This was a good old-fashioned lockdown.

He looked around again: already, lights were going on in upstairs windows and he watched as police teams ran over towards the stairwells and disappeared into the darkness. Within seconds, uniforms had appeared on the upper landings and Blizzard nodded his approval. For several minutes, the inspector did not move, letting events unfold around him, standing and listening to the noises of the raid, the shouted warnings of police officers, the tearing sound of doors being smashed down using hydraulic rams and the enraged bellows of arrested men. Glancing up, the inspector smiled broadly as he saw Colley sprinting across one of the landings, closely followed by Ramsey. He knew that both officers had been looking forward to the operation ever since the chief constable had given it official sanction. Blizzard chuckled as he saw the detectives disappear briefly then re-emerge, manhandling a protesting skinhead.

'Boys will be boys,' he murmured.

Within a few minutes, the first suspects found themselves being brought down the stairs and out into the square where they were frogmarched towards the waiting vans. Blizzard noticed that one of the first to emerge was the youth who had given him the finger after spitting at the patrol car on Sunday afternoon. The inspector held out a hand to the uniformed officer who was holding him.

'I want a word with this one,' he said softly and looked at the bewildered youth. 'If I hear that you are involved in anything dodgy, son, I personally will make sure that they throw the book at you. Never, ever give me the finger again.'

The youth looked at him with fearful eyes, all bluster and bravado banished. Blizzard gave a thin smile: in that moment, he knew that the balance of power had shifted on The Spur. Having watched the youth being bundled into the back of a van, the inspector turned to see Colley walking towards him, the sergeant still with tight hold of the shaven-headed man. Behind them came Ramsey, clutching a plastic bag and grinning broadly.

'Who's he?' asked Blizzard, nodding at the glowering man.

'Robby Jacobs,' said the sergeant. 'Esteemed drug dealer of this parish.'

'And this,' said Ramsey, holding up the bag, 'would seem to be his heroin. Isn't that unfortunate for our Mr Jacobs?'

'Indeed it is,' said the inspector. 'Excellent. Chuck him in the van.'

'Oh, Fee will be down in a minute,' said Ramsey as the sergeant took the arrested man away. 'You should have seen her go – this huge bloke tried to get away from her and before you knew it, she had him down on the ground, squealing like a pig, arm twisted round his back. Scary woman.'

'Tell me about it,' grinned Blizzard.

'Anyway,' said Ramsey, 'can't stop and chat. Got scumbags to arrest.'

Blizzard chuckled as the inspector jogged off to hand the bag of heroin to a uniformed officer then turned and headed back for one of the stairwells, a look of eager anticipation on his face.

'Going well, then,' said Ronald, lumbering up to the inspector as more shouts rent the night air from one of the upper landings. 'The locals certainly seem to be hacked off about something. Can't think what that might be.'

'Neither can I. Hey up, that's tasty,' and Blizzard pointed to a couple of armed officers walking towards them, holding up two shotguns. 'I wouldn't mind betting that they were used in that robbery at the Kingston Road supermarket. Ramsey was pretty sure that someone on The Spur supplied the weapons. They've found all sorts in the other quadrangles.'

'Good stuff,' said the superintendent, rubbing his hands together in glee. 'Think of the effect on the crime figures.'

Blizzard gave him a look.

'No need to turn your nose up, my boy,' said Ronald. 'Targets, always think targets. I've got the monthly meeting on Friday and this will come in extremely useful. Extremely useful indeed. Shut up a few stuffed shirts.'

'Hang on, aren't you a stuffed shirt?'

Before they could continue the conversation, Fee emerged with her quarry, manhandling the large man across the square towards them.

'Evening, sir,' she said to Ronald and headed for the nearest van.

Ronald was about to say something when a particularly loud smashing sound from one of the upper landings attracted their attention and the detectives looked up to see a scuffle taking place between a number of uniformed officers and a couple of burly men. As they watched, the officers gained the upper hand and within moments, the men were being dragged across the quadrangle and placed in vans. Chris Ramsey jogged over to talk to one of the uniforms.

'Who were they, Chris?' asked Blizzard as he returned.

'Another couple of drug dealers. Found some cocaine this time.'

'Good stuff.' Blizzard nodded his approval. 'Those shotguns, do you reckon they were from your Kingston Avenue job?'

'I'd like to think so. Oh, before I forget, Wendy Talbot has been on: they have nicked Barry Roberts in Sheffield and, get this, a couple of lads from The Spur who were actually in the act of delivering knock-off gear.'

The detective inspector headed off to rejoin the fray. By now, crowds of people had gathered on the landings, many roused from their beds by the noise. Round the edges of the square there were ugly murmurings as officers continued to bring out arrested men. Blizzard glanced round and saw Colley ambling over, blood dribbling from a cut on his cheek. The sergeant was speaking earnestly into his mobile phone.

'You OK?' asked the inspector, eyeing the wound with concern.

'Absolutely fine,' said the sergeant, his eyes bright in the blue light thrown from the ranks of police vehicles. 'Let's get on with it.'

'Don't you need to get that seen to?' asked the inspector, gesturing to the gash, then looking at Ronald. 'Don't I need to fill in a health and safety at work form before he can go back to lifting villains?'

'Much as I am a great adherent of paperwork, I think we can cut a corner on this one. Just this once, mind.'

'Besides,' grinned Colley. 'You should see the other guy. His nose will look straight but only if he leans to one side.'

Blizzard roared with laughter.

'Oh, and that was Danny on the phone,' said Colley 'They've lifted George Haywood. He's on his way into Abbey Road. Seemed really shocked that he'd been arrested. Danny reckons he'll talk pretty easily.'

'In which case,' sighed Blizzard, glancing up at Rafferty's flat and noticing a movement of the curtains, 'I guess it's time we got this over with.'

Together, the officers walked across the square and up the stairs until they emerged on to the landing. Without speaking, they walked past a group of uniformed officers who were marching a struggling man out of his flat. A group of youths came out of another flat and defiantly barred the detectives' path. The inspector recognized the youth who had confronted him the last time he was on the estate, the one who had leaned over the balustrade and hurled the insult about Kenny Jarvis. For a brief moment, their eyes met.

'Not so big now, are we, son?' said Blizzard through thin lips.

'I'll have you for this – I know where you fucking live!'

'Unfortunately, I know where you live as well,' said the inspector, bringing his face close to the youth's again. 'Just take a look around you, look at all those police officers and ask yourself who's the one who should be bricking himself?'

He glanced behind him and saw a number of uniformed officers closing in.

'If you and your little mates don't move in the next two seconds,' said Blizzard, 'I'll have you all nicked. And who knows what we might find when we search your flats?'

The youths stepped aside. Blizzard walked past them and knocked on Tommy Rafferty's door. After what seemed like an age, the door opened and Rafferty stood there, his eyes wide with fear when he saw the inspector and his sergeant.

'Blizzard,' said Rafferty nervously, 'what the Hell is happening?'

'A little social visit, Tommy.'

'Well make it look good,' hissed Rafferty. 'I don't want people to think that I gave you information about what—'

'Tommy Rafferty,' said the inspector, 'I am arresting you on suspicion of involvement with the murders of William Guthrie and Roland Turner. That good enough for you?'

Rafferty's mouth fell open.

'Take him away,' said the inspector to the uniforms who had entered the flat. He noticed a figure lurking at the living room door. 'Ah, two for the price of one. Good evening, Steven. I was rather hoping that I might find you here. I think we need a little chat, don't you?'

'What about?' said McGarrity, stepping forward and giving a forced smile.

'You know damned well what about!' exclaimed Blizzard. 'Playing me for a fool, that's what it's about.'

'I have no idea what—'

'We've arrested George Haywood,' said Colley.

McGarrity dropped the can he was holding. Blizzard watched the beer making rivers along the hallway.

'I think,' said the inspector quietly, 'that the party might just be over.'

'Jesus Christ,' breathed McGarrity and slumped against the wall, his face drained of colour.

Blizzard glanced back to where more uniformed officers were waiting.

'Get them out of here,' he said.

Following the two arrested men out on to the landing, Blizzard saw Ramsey walking towards him.

'How's it going?' asked the chief inspector.

'The paperwork will keep us going for weeks. I may even have to colour code it.' Ramsey gave a broad grin. 'Bloody marvellous.'

'Glad you're enjoying yourself,' said Blizzard.

He continued along the landing towards the stairs, a broad smile on his face. The inspector was following his officers down the stairs when shouting erupted in the quadrangle as a youth broke free of his captors. Staring round wildly, he lashed out at the nearest uniform, catching the constable in the face. The officer screamed in pain and staggered backwards and the youth dashed up the nearest stairs. Half-way down, Blizzard could hear the boy's pounding feet and seconds later, the terrified teenager emerged out of the gloom on to the middle landing.

'Come on, son,' said the inspector, holding out a hand. 'It's pointless running.'

There was a glint of steel in the darkness and a knife appeared in the teenager's hand. Blizzard gave a cry and threw up an arm to protect himself but he was too slow and the weapon slashed into his shoulder. The inspector felt a sudden pain shoot down his arm and, with a grunt, he sank to his knees, his mind reeling as he felt the pain coming in relentless waves. Lying in the stinking stairwell, staring up at the ceiling and hearing voices coming as if from afar, Blizzard was vaguely aware of Colley wrestling the youth to the ground and the clink of the knife falling on to the concrete steps. Lying there, drifting in and out of consciousness, Blizzard saw images of Kenny Jarvis's smiling face flashing before his eyes. It was the last thing he remembered.

The square fell silent as the ambulance crew brought an unconscious Blizzard out of the stairwell on a stretcher, accompanied by Fee Ellis, who clung on to his hand as she fought back the tears. The stretcher was borne through the ranks of police officers and loaded carefully into the ambulance. No one spoke: many of the officers had been there the night a similar scene was enacted as the body of Kenny Jarvis was taken away. Even the estate's residents had been stunned into silence. The ambulance edged its way past the police vehicles and vans and out through the tunnel and into the orange glow of the street lights on the main road. As it disappeared into the night, its blue lights flashing, Ronald stood with a gaggle of detectives, feeling an emptiness deep within. He and Blizzard went back twenty-five years and the superintendent recalled the many times he had said to the inspector 'do you know, my life would be a lot better without the aggravation you cause me'. He knew now, knew every time he said it, that nothing could be further from the truth. The superintendent turned and saw Colley.

'You OK?' asked Ronald.

Colley nodded but could find no words: he turned away lest the superintendent see him crying.

'How is he?' asked a voice and Ronald turned to see Brian Robertshaw walking towards him.

'The medics reckoned the knife went in quite deep.'

'I hope he's OK,' said Robertshaw. 'He gave us some pride back tonight.'

'It's a high price to pay for it,' said Ronald, glancing round at the ranks of silent and grim-faced police officers. 'A high price indeed.'

It was a subdued David Colley who walked through the custody suite at Abbey Road shortly before 9 a.m., having gone home to snatch a couple of hours' sleep before making the weary journey back to the police station. He had not slept much, his disturbed dreams full of images of Blizzard on that stretcher. Glancing at the cells, the sergeant sighed. He knew that this should be a jubilant occasion, that in just an hour's work, Western Division had sent shockwaves rippling through the city's criminal fraternity. That this was probably Blizzard's finest moment, his crowning achievement.

The raid had indeed been an outstanding success, the main story on the regional news, and had featured on national television. The chief constable had given numerous interviews, in each of which he had praised the courage of Blizzard but had given little update on his condition. Colley paused to survey the cells: locked behind the grey doors were a number of men who had come to think of themselves as untouchable down the years, who had laughed in the face of the police, but who were now under no illusion that the police had the power and the will to move against their criminal adversaries.

'Result, guv,' murmured Colley.

As he approached the custody desk, a grey-haired

uniformed officer looked at him anxiously from behind the counter.

'How's your gaffer?' asked the custody sergeant.

'Still no word,' said Colley.

'You there when it happened, I think.'

'We'd just got a couple of prisoners down into the yard when this scroat made a break for it. Next thing I know, Blizzard's down and the kid's waving his knife around and threatening to take the rest of us with him.'

'I've got him in 9. The kid's cacking himself.'

'I'll bet he is. He's only seventeen, for God's sake.'

'Heard you took him down. You'll get a commendation for that.'

'Not sure it counts for much,' said Colley and walked out of the custody suite.

'Send Blizzard our regards,' shouted the officer after him. 'Tell him all uniform are thinking about him.'

Colley turned and gave a slight smile.

'Thanks for that,' he said. 'It'll mean a lot to him.'

Colley wandered up the stairs and through the corridors, stopping numerous times to answer the queries from concerned officers wanting to know how Blizzard was. As he approached the CID room, the sergeant saw Arthur Ronald coming the other way.

'Any news, sir?'

'Nothing definite.'

'If only I'd got to him quicker,' said the sergeant, slamming a fist against the wall. 'If only I'd—'

'Ah, if only, if only, Sergeant. I could solve every problem in the world with if only. If only I hadn't told him to get us on to the estate, if only he'd not wanted to arrest Rafferty himself, if only, if only. But don't worry,' and Ronald gave a slight smile and started walking down the corridor, 'John Blizzard is a tough cookie. I wouldn't write him off too quickly.'

Colley watched him go. Was there, he asked himself, just the slightest hint of a jaunty swing in the big man's walk? At a time like this? Colley shook his head to dismiss the idea and walked into the squad room, taking a seat at his desk and staring moodily out of the window. The atmosphere was sombre as over the next few minutes the team reassembled, bleary-eyed, weary of step, each one sitting at their desks trying to look busy but unable to concentrate on their work: there were other, more worrying things to think about and there had been no news from the hospital for four hours. None of them spoke: it did not seem the time. Shortly after 9.30, Chris Ramsey walked into the office and surveyed the gloomy scene.

'OK,' he said, clapping his hands briskly, 'I know we are all worried but we have work to do and Blizzard would not want us to sit here moping on his behalf. We have plenty of bodies in the cells and the custody sergeant wants to know what we are doing with them. So, what I suggest—'

His voice tailed off as there came the faint sound of applause from downstairs. Ramsey looked bemused.

'So, what we need to do—' he began again.

His voice tailed off once more as the applause grew louder, swelling and ebbing until it seemed to fill the whole building. And now there were cheers, cheers which grew louder with every passing second.

'What the—?' said Ramsey, turning to see the figure of John Blizzard standing in the doorway.

Blizzard, right arm in a sling, face slighter paler than usual, glanced at Ramsey's position at the front of the room and gave a slight smile.

'You jump into my grave as quickly?' he said.

Ramsey stood aside, his face a mask of confusion.

'Guv,' he gasped, 'we thought you would be away for ages.'

'Daft basket discharged himself,' said Fee with a disbelieving shake of the head as she followed the chief inspector into the room and the excited officers crowded round him.

'Well, what do you expect?' said Blizzard, sitting down at one of the desks and wincing at the pain from his arm. 'I've always hated quacks and this one reckoned I would be off work for three weeks. Three weeks, I said? Are you mad? I've got a job to do.'

Colley saw a beaming Arthur Ronald walk into the room.

'You knew, sir?' asked the sergeant.

'The lad who works in A & E is an old friend of mine. Rang me up to see if I couldn't talk some sense into Blizzard. I told him I'd been trying to do that for twenty-five years.'

'Besides,' said Blizzard, gingerly patting his injured arm, 'it's not as bad as it looked at the time. Now then, where are we, Chris?'

'Well,' said Ramsey, recovering from his surprise and reaching on to a desk for some papers, 'in the end, we arrested twenty-nine people. The CPS reckon we can get an attempted murder on the lad who attacked you.'

'Not sure about that,' said Blizzard, turning to look at Ronald with a doubtful expression on his face. 'I reckon he just panicked.'

'Well, they want to throw the book at him,' said Ramsey, referring once more to the piece of paper. 'Nine others will be charged with drugs offences, most of in relation to smack. Two will be charged with illegal possession of a firearm – looks like I was right about them being used in the Kingston Avenue job, that just about wraps that one up – and the rest will be charged with assorted lesser offences. All apart from one who we released: we had only arrested him to stop him being such an irritating little git.'

'That not an offence then?' asked Blizzard.

'Fraid not.'

'Jesus,' sighed the inspector, glancing at Ronald. 'You take a couple of hours off and the whole criminal justice system collapses. Anything to link any of them to the RCS inquiry?'

'Plenty. We found the lad who was up on the roof with Terry Roberts when he fell. Reckons they had been told that the train, sorry, the locomotive,' Blizzard nodded his appreciation at the inspector's correction of himself, 'had lots of fittings worth half-inching.'

'Told by whom?' asked Blizzard.

'Your mate Rafferty, it would seem.'

Blizzard nodded gloomily.

'What's more,' continued Ramsey, 'there's a strong suspicion that Jacobs was one of the lads who killed Billy Guthrie and did for Roly Turner.'

'Where are McGarrity and the others now?'

'In the cells. It's a good job you're back, they say they'll only talk to you.'

'In which case,' said Blizzard, getting up and holding his arm as the pain shot through it, 'I'd better do just that.'

'You going to be OK?' asked Ronald.

Blizzard nodded. As the chief inspector reached the door, Ramsey took a step forward.

'Guv?' he said.

Blizzard turned round.

'Yes?'

'I would just like to say that I, that is we, all of us,' and Ramsey glanced round the room, 'are really glad to see you back. You had us worried for a moment.'

Blizzard gave a half-smile but said nothing and walked slowly out into the corridor. Left behind in the squad room, the detectives listened as there came the sound of applause again as the chief inspector walked along the corridors and down the stairs to the custody suite.

'Ok,' said Ramsey, turning to face the others, 'I guess we ought to get on with some work.'

Movement returned to the room.

chapter twenty

Blizzard sat at the desk in the stuffy little interview room and stared at the gaunt, broken figure of Steve McGarrity. With his arm throbbing, the inspector tried hard to focus on the job in hand, to push emotion to the back of his mind, to forget that Steve McGarrity was a friend. *Had* been a friend. Sitting next to him, Colley kept glancing at his colleague with concern.

'You OK?' he whispered.

'Yeah, but let's get this over with quickly.'

McGarrity, who had been staring at the floor ever since the officers had arrived, looked up at his old friend.

'I heard you got hurt,' he said, nodding to the sling. 'What happened?'

'Kid knifed me.'

'Tough place, The Spur.'

'Which is why I am wondering how an upstanding citizen like you got involved in its ways,' said Blizzard. 'I mean, what were you thinking of, Steve? A man like you?'

'We had nowhere to go,' he shrugged. 'We needed help and The Spur could offer it.'

'So tell me about Matthew Hargreaves.'

McGarrity looked at him for a moment: the detectives wondered if he was preparing to bluster out their questions but he gave a defeated nod of the head.

'How much do you know?' he asked.

'Enough to be pretty certain that you were partly responsible for his death.'

'You get that from the others?'

'Got it from George Haywood. Tommy's saying nothing but he knows the game's up.'

McGarrity considered the comment. For a moment or two, it seemed as if he might break down and cry but the old railman regained his composure and nodded.

'This was not supposed to happen, none of it was supposed to happen,' he said. 'He was a good man, was Matthew Hargreaves.'

'But not a good union man?'

'No, not a good union man.' McGarrity looked hard at the detectives. 'Before you judge me, us, out of hand, you have to understand what those times were like. It's not as straightforward as you think, John.'

'That's DCI Blizzard to you.'

McGarrity sighed.

'Yes,' he said, 'I guess it is.'

'So explain what was happening at those times,' said Colley.

'You know what the mid-eighties were like,' said McGarrity. 'The miners' strike had not long finished.'

'I remember the miners' strike,' nodded Colley. 'I was one of those bussed over to Yorkshire to help out on the picket line. Scary.'

'Aye, there was a lot of strong emotions stirred up. Friend set against friend. It was the way of things at the time and it were the same when we had our strike.'

'Over what?' asked Blizzard.

'It was a local dispute over changes in shift patterns. We were in the thick of it. I was the branch secretary, George Haywood was the treasurer and Tommy Rafferty was one of the leading lights on the committee. He were a right rabble-rouser in them days.'

'And you were out how long?'

'Nine weeks. They had to bring in scab labour to keep the railways running. You should have seen the picket lines when they bussed these lads in.' McGarrity shook his head. 'Like you said, Sergeant, it was scary.'

'But Matthew Hargreaves did not go out with your members, I think?' said Blizzard.

'He did at first but then he said he was not prepared to countenance all the violence. He was a good Christian lad, was Matty Hargreaves.'

'What violence?'

'A couple of the scabs were beaten up one night. Ended up in hospital. Nowt to do with us, it was down to a gang of flying pickets from Donny, spotted them in a pub on their way home.'

'So Hargreaves went back on principle?'

'Yeah. Madness, he knew what would happen.'

'I was talking to an old friend of mine, works with the Transport Police. He reckons that Hargreaves had his windows put out.'

'Happened on the first night after he went back to work,' nodded McGarrity. 'He had to move his wife and kid in with her mother but that were nothing to do with us, honest.'

'But what happened next was?'

'More Tommy, really. The strike was getting more bitter by the day – management were taking a hard line – and we became so angry seeing Matty Hargreaves walking into work every day that, well, you know how it is.'

'So you approached Billy Guthrie?'

'Yeah, he'd only just been sacked by the railways for nicking so he bore them a grudge anyway. Not that he needed much of an excuse to beat someone up. Anyway, when I told him that Hargreaves had taken the side of the bosses, that was enough. You know what happened next.'

'Guthrie attacked Hargreaves in the yard.'

'Yeah. Just to rough him up, you know, put the frighteners on. Get him to go back on strike.' McGarrity looked hopefully at Blizzard. 'You have to believe that. We never meant for him to die. Besides, it worked: when he came out of hospital, Hargreaves did go back on strike. And he never told no one who attacked him. Then not longer after, Guthrie did his vanishing act.'

'I bet you were delighted,' grunted Blizzard.

'It didn't really change much. We spent years waiting for the knock on the door from your lot then last week up pops Billy Guthrie like a bad penny, talking soft about wanting to say sorry to folks. Came to see me Thursday night. Said he did not want to do it but his partner had insisted on it, otherwise she would put him in a home when he became too ill. Said she had a sister in Hafton so she would know if he didn't go through with it. I tell you, it was the first time I ever saw Billy Guthrie afeared of anything.'

'What did he want with you?'

'Said he was looking for Joe Hargreaves. Would I help him find him?'

'So you decided to silence him?'

'What could we do?' McGarrity looked helplessly at Blizzard. 'Guthrie knew he was taking a risk but he hadn't changed, he was sure that you'd never get a case to stick after all these years. But we were terrified. Folks were already talking about Guthrie being back and we reckoned it was only a matter of time before word got back to you and we got dragged into it. None of us would have lasted a week in prison.'

'But you didn't do the actual killing?'

'What, at our age?' McGarrity allowed himself a slight

smile. 'No. Tommy had a word with Terry Roberts and he sorted it. Got some lads from the estate.'

'We've got one of them already,' said Colley. 'Bloke called Jacobs. He's named three others as well.'

'No honour among thieves, eh?' murmured McGarrity.

'So where does Megan Rees fit in with it?' asked Blizzard.

'Guthrie had been banging on about wanting to say sorry to her about what happened to her dad. We told him that she would be at the wasteland, said she worked in a pub nearby and she got off late. Guthrie turned up at midnight and Terry Roberts's lads did the rest. Then we told Megan where she could find his body.'

'Why on earth do that?'

'George had known her dad – reckoned Megan would want to see Guthrie's body.'

'But wasn't that taking a risk?' asked Blizzard. 'What if she had turned you in?'

'She wouldn't have done that.'

'How do you know?'

McGarrity paused. 'I just know,' he said.

'But why on earth did she dial 999? Surely that would only draw attention to herself?'

'She wasn't meant to report the body but a young couple saw her in the signal box. She had no option. It would have attracted more suspicion if you had had to trace her.'

'And why place the death notice in the paper?' asked Blizzard.

'We thought if it read like someone out for revenge, you wouldn't even look at us. Besides, we never thought you'd trace it back to us. The credit card had been nicked by one of the lads on The Spur and Jacobs got his girlfriend to use it to place the notice with the paper. She pretended to be a relative of Guthrie. The niece or something.'

'One thing I don't understand,' said Colley. 'If Megan Rees

was in on what you were doing, why on earth did you frame her?'

'We didn't.'

'What about the credit card we found on the wasteland?'

'Jacobs dropped it, the daft bastard,' said McGarrity with a disbelieving shake of the head, 'Then when he realized it must be on the wasteland, it was too late and he dare not go back to look for it in case someone saw him.'

'So Megan Rees was innocent?' said Colley.

'She had nowt to do with it,' said McGarrity firmly.

Blizzard said nothing.

'And these lads who killed Guthrie,' asked Colley. 'How did you persuade them to get involved?'

'Paid them two hundred quid each and we told Terry Roberts about the Old Lady. Tommy knew that Roberts was nicking stuff for his uncle to fence over in Sheffield. Roberts loved the idea of nicking stuff from the locomotive – think of the newspaper headlines, he said. He kept all his newspaper cuttings, did Terry Roberts. Said he'd love to see your face.'

'How could you?' murmured Blizzard. 'I mean, all those hours we spent working on her?'

'Like I always said,' shrugged McGarrity, 'only you got carried away with all that romance stuff. To the rest of us, it was just a job and not a very good one at that. That's why we went on strike.'

'And all that guff about Lawrie Gaines?'

'Guthrie had banged on about him as well, said he had arranged to see him on the Friday. It all fitted beautifully. I knew that Eddie Gayle has been involved in fixing fights on the night Archie got hurt and I reckoned you would love that. Thought it would keep you busy for a long time. Never reckoned you would suspect us and, let's be fair, we'd have got away with it if Joe Hargreaves had kept his trap shut.'

'And he might have done if you hadn't had Roly Turner killed,' said Blizzard.

'We didn't mean for him to die.'

'Who attacked him?'

'The same lads as did for Guthrie, I assume. Jacobs sorted it. We heard that Roly had been to see Joe and guessed what it was about – he'd mentioned to one or two people that he wondered if Guthrie's death was linked to the attack on Matty. The idea was for the boys to persuade him to keep quiet and tell Joe the same. We didn't know he had a bad heart.' McGarrity paused then looked at the detectives, his eyes moist with tears as his composure broke. 'He was a good man was Roly.'

'Jesus Christ,' sighed Blizzard, the pain in his arm suddenly intensifying. 'What a mess.'

McGarrity shrugged. 'Sorry,' he said.

The inspector stood up and walked from the room followed by the sergeant. Once outside in the corridor, Blizzard leaned against the wall and closed his eyes.

'I've been such a fool,' he groaned. 'All that rubbish about how wonderful railmen are.'

'Maybe,' said Colley, looking at him sympathetically, 'all you did was forget that they were real people.'

Blizzard looked at him for a moment then nodded his head.

'Maybe you're right,' he said. 'Maybe you're right.'

chapter twenty-one

After lunch, and suddenly starting to feel weary as the events of the past twenty-four hours caught up with him and his arm started to throb incessantly, Blizzard decided to go home early. He was about to leave the office when a call came through from reception.

'Sorry, sir,' said a girl's voice, 'but Eddie Gayle is here with his lawyer. Says he wants to see you to demand an apology.'

'Tell him to wait,' said the inspector, struggling into his jacket.

With a slight smile on his face, he headed down the corridor. Two minutes later, he walked slightly unsteadily out into the back yard of the station, supported on Fee's arm. As they approached the constable's car, Fee looked up and noticed a figure in jeans and a green jacket standing in the belt of trees behind the barrier.

'Megan Rees,' said Fee. 'I'll go and see what she wants.'

'We'll both go.'

The detectives walked over and ducked beneath the barrier.

'Megan?' said Blizzard, noticing the strange expression on her face. 'Are you OK?'

'The radio said you got them,' she said. 'The men who killed Billy Guthrie.'

'It would seem so. I'm sorry for what you had to go through.'

'Maybe I'm as guilty as them.'

'How come?' said Blizzard, moving a couple of steps further away and motioning for Fee to do the same, the constable having also sensed the sudden tension in the atmosphere.

'How come you are as guilty as them?' repeated Blizzard.

'Like I said, there was not a day gone past when I did not want to murder Billy Guthrie.'

'Yes, but there's a big difference between thinking it and doing it, Megan.'

'Who do think put the idea into their heads?' she said with a slight smile. 'Do you really think they are bright enough to think of it by themselves?'

The detectives stared at her.

'Are you saying—?' began Blizzard.

'That I planned it all? Yes. Billy Guthrie rang me and said he wanted to apologize. I agreed to meet him at the signal box. Getting McGarrity and the others involved was easy. They'd have done anything to keep themselves out of prison for what they did to Matty Hargreaves.'

'But how did you know about that?'

'My dad … found it in his papers after he died. He'd been a good friend of George Haywood when they worked on the railways. One night, they got drunk and Haywood told him what had happened. I don't know why, but Dad wrote it all down. Put it in a sealed envelope in the dresser.'

'So how come nobody has mentioned you in their interviews?' asked Blizzard.

'Perhaps they don't think that prison is a suitable place for a nice girl like me,' she said with a slight smile. 'Salt of the earth, these old railmen, you know.'

'Are you sure this is not just some delusion? I mean, you do have a history of mental illness.'

'Now that,' said Megan, 'is for you to find out.'

Fee suddenly noticed that she was clutching the newspaper cutting out of which smiled the constable's face.

'What have you got that for?' she asked sharply.

'I was going to kill him.'

'Kill who?' asked the inspector.

'I was going to kill you.' Megan delivered the line in a matter-of-fact way.

'Why would you do that?' exclaimed Blizzard.

'My dog died.' Megan looked at the appalled expression on Fee's face. 'I wanted your little girlfriend to know what it was like to lose someone as well.'

She reached into her jacket and produced a kitchen knife which she handed to the inspector handle first.

'But I don't think I'll bother now,' she said.

Megan Rees turned and walked back through the trees. Fee made to go after her but Blizzard reached out a restraining hand.

'There's plenty of time for that,' he said.

'But—'

'Besides, I'm in no hurry to tell Myra Randolph that she was right, that Megan Rees really is as mad as a hatter. Get Colley to pick her up.'

He started walking back towards the car.

'Or better still,' he said, 'get Arthur to sort it. Myra Randolph likes him.'

It was just after lunchtime on Saturday that Blizzard arrived at the old shed on the wasteland close to the Railway Hotel. The inspector, his arm still in a sling but with movement rapidly returning, had been dropped off by Fee who had promised to come back for him after she had been shopping in the city centre. The inspector stood in the gloom cast by the naked lightbulb and surveyed the sight before him – the oil-stained floor where the Old Lady had once stood, the tools hanging up on hooks, the cluttered workbenches, the kettle and the box of teabags. Blizzard smiled: after the tumult of the previous week, he suddenly felt at peace. Three days of enforced absence from work had proved increasingly frustrating and he had found himself wandering round the house desperate for something to do. Now, he was delighted to have something to occupy his mind as he set about preparing the shed for the arrival of the railway appreciation society's new locomotive, using his one good arm to tidy up benches and clear away rubbish.

The inspector had only been there a few minutes when the door creaked open and he turned to see Colley carrying Laura, who was dressed all in green apart from a bright red sunhat.

'Fee said I'd find you here,' said the sergeant, glancing round the empty shed. 'Hey, looks a bit sad, doesn't it?'

'Not for long,' beamed Blizzard, grinning even more as Laura reached out a chubby hand towards him.

'I kinda assumed the association would fold after all that's happened.'

'No way,' said the inspector as he and the baby playfully intertwined fingers. 'There's still plenty of us up for some work and yesterday I got a call confirming that we can take an old tank engine which needs doing up.'

'What,' said Colley, looking at the baby and grinning, 'like Thomas? A blue one?'

'Er, yeah, something like that. Anyway, that's what I came down here for, make sure everything is OK for when it arrives. They're due to deliver it on Thursday.'

'Does this mean we can look forward to more tripe about romantic railways then?'

'Ah, no, think I'll keep off that theme for a while, David.'

'Wise strategy, guv.'

There was silence for a moment and Blizzard noticed the sergeant looking at him.

'What's wrong?' asked the inspector.

'Can I ask you a question?'

'Of course.'

Colley looked uncomfortable.

'Come on, spit it out,' said Blizzard.

'OK, it's just that some of the guys have been talking, you know how they do, and we kinda wondered if you were thinking of retiring?'

Blizzard stared at him.

'Retiring?' he said. 'Whatever gave you that idea?'

'You've been talking about it quite a bit lately. Folks have noticed.'

'OK,' said Blizzard after a few moments, 'I have been thinking about it, I'm not getting any younger, but it was only an idle thought and the past three days has put the idea out of my head again. I tell you, I've been so bored. I'd much rather be filling in forms for HR. That should please Arthur.'

'And me.'

There was an awkward silence then Blizzard looked closer at the motif of a beaming purple dinosaur on the front of Laura's romper suit.

'Is that—?' he began.

'Yeah, that's Barnie,' grinned Colley. 'Wondered when you'd notice.'

'Cheerful looking bastard, isn't he?' said Blizzard as Laura looked down at the dinosaur. 'Mind, despite what you had to say about him, I don't reckon he could have killed Terry Roberts, really.'

'Probably not,' chuckled Colley. 'Hey, how's the arm?'

'Getting better,' said the inspector, waggling it round to prove the point.

'Can it throw bread?'

'What?'

'Well, it's a nice summer's afternoon and Jay has kicked us out of the house so I wondered if you fancied coming to the park and feeding some ducks? If you're lucky, I'll buy you an ice cream.'

'Do you know,' said Blizzard with a smile. 'I think I might just do that.'

And the two detectives walked out into the afternoon sunshine.